NO BED C

Recent Titles by Vera Cowie from Severn House

DESIGNING WOMAN
MEMORIES
NO BED OF ROSES
SHADES OF LOVE
THAT SUMMER IN SPAIN

NO BED OF ROSES

Vera Cowie

This first world edition published in Great Britain 2000 by
SEVERN HOUSE PUBLISHERS LTD of
9–15 High Street, Sutton, Surrey SM1 1DF.
This first world edition published in the USA 2000 by
SEVERN HOUSE PUBLISHERS INC of
595 Madison Avenue, New York, N.Y. 10022.

British Library Cataloguing in Publication Data

Cowie, Vera, 1928-
  No bed of roses
  1. Love stories
  I. Title
  823.9'14 [F]

  ISBN 0-7278-5564-6

All situations in this publication are fictitious and
any resemblance to living persons is purely coincidental.

Typeset by Hewer Text Ltd.,
Edinburgh, Scotland.
Printed and bound in Great Britain by
MPG Books Ltd, Bodmin, Cornwall.

One

The impatient slamming of the front door had Fiona on her feet instantly, and, going to the open doorway, she stood four-square in it so that the man striding down the hall towards her had no choice but to see her. She had been waiting a whole forty minutes, after all. But his reaction on seeing her was not that of a guilty man, rather an appreciative one.

"Hello," he said appraisingly, raising eyebrows as blond as his butterball hair. "Who are you?"

Fiona silently handed him her card. He glanced at it before smiling down at her, affably unfazed. "Oh, yeah . . . sure. I apologise for keeping you waiting. I got tied up." He ran the tape-measure of his eyes over her in a thoroughly comprehensive scan that was in no way sexually demeaning, only curious; from the top of her burnished head to the tips of her glossy Kurt Geiger pumps. Fiona had never met eyes quite like them: so light a grey as to be almost colourless, reflecting pools of light in a face that bore the permanent tan of exposure to all weathers, confirmed by the delta of fine lines radiating outwards from the corner of his eyes, evidence of constant narrowing against brilliant sunlight. He was also tall enough to make her tilt her head back so as to be able to look into his face.

"Fiona Sutherland," he read from her card, experimentally, as if testing for flavour. "You Scotch?"

"A Scot. Scotch is what you Americans call our whisky."

She saw the light eyes flare with amusement before he drawled: "I'm a bourbon man myself." Then: "The agency told you the score?"

"Minus three?"

"Not my fault. I was very precise in my specification, besides which I went to them in the first place because I was told they were the outfit to go to if you wanted the best."

"We are, but it's not easy to come up with a combination of Jacqueline Kennedy Onassis, Margaret Thatcher and Sharon Stone."

This time he laughed, throwing his head back in enjoyment, revealing flawless American teeth and causing his butter-yellow hair to shed raindrops. "A fair assessment, but I repeat: I was assured they could find me one. You here to tell me they can't?"

"I *am* the agency and I'm here to tell you that we can."

The pale eyes dazzled, like sun on water. "Now that's what I call service!"

Fiona found her anger had evaporated, unable to burn in the sunny warmth of his charm. His sense of humour so exactly matched her own that she had to firm her quivering lips before saying equally: "The three girls I chose were among my best, so when the latest one threw in the towel I thought it high time I investigated the situation personally."

"Lady, you can investigate me anytime," he assured

2

her earnestly, making it Fiona's turn to laugh. What on earth had those three idiots been thinking of? What was there not to like about this man? Always one to go by first impressions, she found hers to be a mixture of relief (after what she had been told about him) and anticipation (because of what she was learning about him). When he thrust out a hand and said, "J. J. Lucas, but everybody calls me Luke," his handshake was as firm and brisk as he was; no macho crush to prove his masculinity. But then, everything about him was as crisp as a brand-new hundred-dollar bill. He reminded her of nothing so much as a length of rawhide: not an ounce of spare flesh, and what there was in the peak of physical condition. As he took off his wet Burberry to throw it carelessly on to a nearby chair, her estimation of him as a cowboy was confirmed: narrow-legged jeans held up by a leather belt studded with ornate silver ornaments and fastened with a huge buckle, plus a blue and white checked shirt. All that was missing, she thought, was the stetson.

"So . . . are you prepared to go to bat?" he asked.

With her knowledge of American-speak, as well as having already made up her mind to do so, she answered him in the same language. "That's why I made it personal. I'm here to see if you would be prepared to let me give it a whirl."

Another lift of the expressive blond brows. "You mean you're able to leave your own business to help me run mine?"

"I am fortunate enough to have an assistant who is a combination of Henry Kissinger and Pamela Anderson."

"Then why didn't you send her?"

3

"Because my need is greater than yours."

Another grin. "We won't go into *that* right now!"

Their exchanged smile was totally complicitous. Fiona had already forgotten that he had kept her waiting forty minutes; that she had been determined to treat him with frostbitten politeness; that he had been described to her as a slave driver with a weird household set-up. He was so likeable you were disarmed before you could reach for your weapons, and as comfortable to be with as a favourite pair of old slippers.

"Least I can do to make up for my tardiness is offer you a drink, though I see Henry gave you coffee."

"And a piece of superlative brownie."

"Henry is one of the world's great cooks."

Going over to the big cabinet that stood against one wall, he opened it to display every alcoholic drink known to man. "What will you have?"

"A gin and tonic, please."

Watching him expertly make her an ice-laden American glassful, with a twist of lime rather than lemon, she noticed that he was as deft with his hands as he was with his tongue. Handing over her drink, he turned back to the cabinet to pour enough Jack Daniels to cover the rocky mountain of ice in his own glass, then waited until she had seated herself in one of the big suede-upholstered chairs before folding his long length into a matching one. Fiona mentally marked her score card: manners 10; personality 10; punctuality . . . well, she would give him the benefit of the doubt and a 2. Taking a deep swallow of her drink, she found it to be just right.

"So . . ." he asked easily, propping one ankle on his

other knee, "what's the story on you taking things personally?"

But Fiona was gazing in fascination at his feet. He was wearing cowboy boots: high-heeled, well worn but lovingly cared for, the leather a faded gold and soft as silk, tooled into a swirling pattern with a hot iron, showing signs of wear only around the heels, where spurs had rubbed.

Noticing her stare, "Best thing in the world on a horse," he advised affably. "You ride?"

"Not in London."

"I do – whenever and wherever I can, in fact."

Fiona found herself saying: "Was that what held you up? Hog-tying steers?"

His laugh was genuine, but: "Easy on the spurs," he advised. "To get back to the matter in hand, what was it the other girls complained of?"

"I don't think they felt up to – er – life in the no-speed-limit fast lane," Fiona extemporised, which did not begin to cover the indignant tirade of Penny Latymer, the last of the trio and an experienced, highly competent thirty-five-year-old. "It is just not on, Miss Sutherland. I've worked in some odd set-ups in my time, but this one is really peculiar. You're expected to function like a state-of-the-art computer during the day then, if he is wining and dining in the pursuit of business, you're expected to come on like Marilyn Monroe, no matter how dog-tired you are, and believe me, he is tireless! Some days you don't set eyes on him, others he's at it for ten hours or more, straight off the bat, at the end of which you're in no fit state to charm anybody! Why can't he get one of his own women to act as his hostess? God knows they're decorative enough!"

"His *own* women?"

"Yes, his harem. All built to the same specification. Blonde, blue-eyed and empty-headed, tending to hug the curves. He changes them along with his sheets." Indignation in full spate: "I would not call myself a prude, Miss Sutherland" (which means I would, thought Fiona), "but it is a *most* unconventional household, to say the least. An Oklahoma cowboy who just happens to be one of *Fortune*'s 500, which means he is seriously – and I mean *seriously* – rich; a partner who is also his lawyer who just happens to be a Native American called Charlie Whitesky; and a black American who cooks gourmet meals of the kind that would ruin any woman's figure in a week and purses his lips when you don't clear your plate!" Her headshake was all outraged convention. "It is just not *me*, Miss Sutherland, and I don't feel I can give of my best where I don't feel comfortable. I'd prefer the kind of assignment I am used to."

Fiona, who had been born insatiably curious – her father used to say her first words were "how", "who", "why", "where" and "when" – marvelled at such hidebound conventionality, but then, Penny thought "imagination" was the title of a song by John Lennon, while her sense of humour only ever saw jokes by appointment. Therefore the picture she had painted had to be from life, which was when Fiona knew she would make it her business to go along and take a good look at it for herself. She had to, because the painting contained a Native American. All her life she had been fascinated by the people who had, as Will Rogers (part Cherokee himself) said, met the boat when the *Mayflower* docked. Ever since she had read *The Last of the Mohicans* at the age of eleven she had made it her business to learn all she could about the people: Cheyenne, Sioux, Arapahoe, Blackfeet, Crow, Apache, Kiowa, all the tribal nations once known – in pre-politically correct days – as Red Indians. As soon as she was free to do so, she had made the first of several pilgrimages to the American West to see for herself the places of their legends. She had read deeply and voraciously about their history, their practices and beliefs, the intricate differences between tribes, even between bands in tribes; she relished their way of life, their folklore. She grieved at how shamefully they had been treated by the American Bureau of Indian Affairs, when the advancing white man had taken away their land, massacred their vital buffalo and broken every treaty they ever signed, along with the promises they made. To have the chance actually to *work* with and for a Native American was one not to be missed. She could *really* learn then.

"Nothing ever gets any place in the slow lane; it takes too long," J. J. Lucas was saying. "If I am demanding it's because my work is too. I've no doubt you already know that my principal interest is oil: Lucas Oil is where I made – still make – most of my money, but I have a lot of other interests, and they take a deal of keeping up with. I dabble in venture capital; I own bits and pieces of a lot of other companies and I like to keep track of how they're doing, so you have to know your way around the financial pages and understand what you read, marking

7

any fluctations you think I should know about. You will
have to familiarise yourself with my database, and know
how to create the necessary graphics because I do regular
presentations to clients on site findings. The pressure is
always set to high, but I don't ask of others what I am not
prepared to give myself. The hours can be long; if I have
to go anywhere at short notice I expect you to hold the
fort, but I don't mind if, once you've done what has to be
done, you sit and read or file your nails or whatever. Just
so long as you're within reach of the phone, the fax and
the e-mail at all times. That's why I pay well over the
going rate." He eyed her. "Still interested?"

"Fascinated."

Sipping his bourbon, he asked, "You married?"

"No."

"Engaged?"

"No."

"Boyfriend?"

"No."

The expressive eyebrows lifted in surprise, but he said:
"That suits me. I need someone who can keep their mind
on their work – and me – twenty-four hours a day, which
is why I want someone to live in. The phone goes day and
night, and so do I, and if I have not only to make an
instant decision but act on it the same way, I need the
right person on the spot to do what is necessary. I don't
work to live, Ms Sutherland, but I do live to work. You
prepared to take that on?"

"I am not afraid of hard work."

Their eyes met and held. He would test her mettle,
Fiona knew, but she found the prospect exhilarating

rather than frightening. She did not lack confidence in her own abilities. He was providing her with fair warning that he would give no quarter, which made her all the more determined never to ask for any.

He surveyed her thoughtfully for a moment longer then suddenly he smiled, a strangely sweet smile which changed the narrow, fine-boned face into something oddly vulnerable. "OK, then. Let me show you where it all happens."

Draining his glass, he set it down before uncoiling his length from his chair. He had the longest legs Fiona had ever seen on any man. They went on for ever, comprising two-thirds of his body, which was long too. He had narrow hips but the shoulders under the checked shirt were broad. Fiona had no difficulty imagining him in the saddle – an American saddle, of course – ready to roll himself in his blanket and get a good night's sleep on the unforgiving ground.

Utterly bemused by now, she followed him down the length of the enormous, expensively and luxuriously furnished split-level sitting room, all cream and gold, coffee and yellow, to where he was holding open a jib-door set immediately under the balcony of the upper level. She stepped through into a high, wide and handsome room, airy with the light that fell through a wall of windows curtained in filmy voile and overlooking the oval of The Boltons. Fiona thought with a wince of what the rent must be, sure that only someone with a *very* deep pocket would be able to afford it.

Examining the room, she saw it was all state-of-the-art and computerised to the nth degree; there was not one but half a dozen of the latest Apple Macs, all with their screens displaying different information: stock-market indexes – the Dow, the Hang Seng, the Nikkei and the Dax among them. Her quick scan took in currency movements, global transactions involving takeovers, information about current trading in international financial centres. There was also a large-screen television set, tuned to the Bloomberg Financial channel, plus several fax machines. Her desk was a minimalist glass slab, and on it she had her own Apple Mac, fax and three telephones. Well, he had said the phone and the fax and the e-mailing never stopped. No wonder. As it was, every fax was displaying messages, which he tore off, read, then either threw away or laid in a big tray marked YES (one of three, the others marked NO and MAYBE) on her desktop.

"Very efficient," Fiona commented appreciatively.

"That's what I'm paying for."

"And that's what you'll get!"

Mentally she thanked her lucky stars that she had recently taken an intensive refresher course in the latest software techniques, including databases, tables, presentations, charts – both pie and bar – cells, queries and File Manager. The way this office was equipped told her she would need them all.

Once again eyes met as they squared off: tall, lean, laconic man; petite, rounded, wholly feminine woman, neat as a pin in her Rive Gauche amethyst tweed suit, an exact match to her extravagantly lashed eyes while complimenting the fine old-burgundy hair coiled sleekly behind the small head. Teak carving as against porcelain Tanagra figurine.

"I do a lot of reports for people who want my advice as to the possibility of oil-bearing sites. I fly to wherever they need me so I can take samples, do tests, calculate costs, provide facts and figures as to whether – if there is oil – the site will be profitable."

"You're a geologist?" The last thing on earth she would have thought him. She had the feeling it was the first of many surprises where this man was concerned.

"Among other things. I've spread my interests the past few years. There is naturally a lot of client contact and I entertain when I deem it necessary. That is where you come in. I do a lot of business over a good dinner – Henry provides that. Your job will be ostensibly to preside as my hostess, but in reality to listen and learn. I need someone with a flypaper memory and a head for figures, because a lot can be divulged after a few glasses of good wine – only I ask that you restrict your own intake so's you don't lose track of what's going on, even if I do. Henry knows about wine. When it comes to housekeeping he knows it all, which is why I give him a free hand. He occupies the third corner of our little triangle. The second one holds my partner, Charlie Whitesky – I say 'partner', but he's one of the silent kind. Lucas Oil belongs to me and I run it, but Charlie is my lawyer, and as such he's in on just about everything so we work in tandem, as they say. Right now he's in Switzerland so you'll meet him later."

He waited, but Fiona said nothing.

"Another thing. I don't keep regular office hours. I go when and where I'm needed, often at a moment's notice. Sometimes you'll come, sometimes not."

"Have passport, will travel," Fiona informed him evenly.

"You'll take me on, then?"

Something in his voice made her answer: "I am sure I can give you what you want."

Once again the light eyes wandered over her. "I don't doubt it for a minute," he murmured. "When can you start?"

"Tomorrow morning?"

"Fine. Bring your things along and Henry will see you settled in. Any questions?"

"Not at this moment."

He nodded. "OK. See you tomorrow, then."

He walked her back into the living room, where she asked: "Would it be possible to call a taxi? I didn't come by car, as parking around here is impossible."

"Sure." Raising his voice to a level that would have reached the King's Road, where her offices were, he bawled: "Henry, call a cab for Ms Sutherland. It's raining like hell out there," while he helped her on with her own Burberry, and handed over her umbrella. The living-room door opened and Henry stuck his head in. "It just so happens I already got one standin' by, right at the front door," he said in dignified tones. "And I ain't deaf, neither."

Fiona shook hands again, then followed Henry.

"Cab's paid for," he told her. "We got an account. You comin' or goin'?"

"I start tomorrow morning," Fiona told him.

"Good. I'll be waitin' on you."

He took her umbrella from her, opened it up and

escorted her to the waiting cab, handing it over only when she was safe inside. Then he nodded and smiled before going back into the house.

Well! thought Fiona, after telling the driver where to go. And well again! Not the usual run of offices, indeed! This ought to be the most interesting assignment I've ever been on, and then some!

She had not been out on a job since she found the demand for her own services exceeded her ability to satisfy them. Then, using the not inconsequential sum of money which came her way following the death of her father, she decided to set up Crème de la Crème, her small, highly selective agency for well-educated, personable, high-powered personal assistants, who had to have well-proven secretarial/organising/managerial skills, fluent command of at least two foreign languages, a minimum of ten years' experience at the chairman or MD level, and to be already earning the high salary commensurate with such skills and experience. She never took on anyone she did not thoroughly first investigate then test, and she did the same deep background checks on her clients. The information she had on J. J. Lucas gave him an AAA+++ rating; said he was an oil-rich entrepreneur who owned Lucas Oil – not one of the Seven Sisters but a highly profitable Getty Oil-type company based in Oklahoma – outright; and had every finger – and probably most of his toes – in an assortment of very profitable pies. He was in Europe for at least six months, most probably a year, and was looking to invest some of his venture capital in whatever took his fancy or promised rich dividends. He was thirty-eight and single, drank but not heavily and usually Jack Daniels, did not smoke, and was a cool-headed but daring gambler, both for business and pleasure. Poker was his preferred game, but he was also known to like blackjack, and the names of the men who had sponsored him at Crockfords and the Clermont had made it plain he was a high roller presently being given the red carpet treatment.

There was no way she could resist this one. Her curiosity, which never slept, was raring to go, and her enquiring mind, which loved nothing more than getting to the bottom of *anything*, knew it would be kept at full stretch. She could safely leave the agency in the capable hands of Sue Ryland, her assistant, who would jump at the chance of running things for a while. She had been Fiona's first "find", so good she had been co-opted to help run the agency.

Oh, yes, Fiona thought gleefully, high on anticipation as the cab turned into the King's Road. She had struck it lucky today. The next few months were going to be absolutely fascinating!

Two

At nine thirty the following morning she presented herself and her two cases at the gleaming front door of the house in The Boltons to find Henry waiting for her. He was a handsome, middle-aged Denzil Washington, deceptively sleepy-eyed, and soft-voiced, with an accent like molasses.

"Mornin'," he greeted her, taking her cases from her and setting them down on the highly polished parquet flooring. "You had breakfast?"

"Coffee only."

"Then come down to the kitchen once you got yourself settled. I just now took some blueberry muffins out the oven."

"Yes, please . . ."

"Right. Your room's on the third floor . . . come ahead and I'll show you."

It was a delight: a king-size bed, a sumptuous dressing table, a wall of mirrors concealing spacious closets, and a sybaritic bathroom adjoining. She quickly unpacked, distributed bottles and jars, hung her robe behind the bathroom door then followed her nose to the lower ground floor and the kitchen.

It was big enough for a hotel: all stainless steel and

gadgetry – all American, Fiona noticed. In the middle of
its hollow, cooking-cum-eating core, Henry was pouring
coffee. "Set yourself down, have a cup of coffee. There's
always coffee day and night in any house where J. J.
Lucas lays his head. He drinks 'bout a gallon a day."

"Where is he?"

"Still sleepin'. He had a late night."

"Entertaining?"

Henry lifted a shoulder. "More like bein' entertained."
His eyes, liquid brown shoepolish, met hers head-on in a
way that had her mentally bracing herself. "She's still
sleepin' too . . ."

Fiona knew she was being tried on for size, so she
merely smiled a none-of-my-business smile and looked
towards the plate of muffins, bursting with juicy blue-
berries.

"Help yourself," Henry invited, and she knew she had
passed.

At the first mouthful she closed her eyes in bliss.
"Mmmmmm . . ."

Henry relaxed. This one would do. He'd had a feelin'
about her ever since he let her through the front door.
Nobody's fool and not totin' prejudices. And the best-
lookin'. Sassy too, according to Luke. "I think we've
landed a Triple Crown winner," he'd said last night.
And, thank God, she was an eater. Nobody who ate with
such relish was a two-bites-and-no-more-thank-you
picky-picky dieter. She was not skinny but she wasn't
fat neither. Just – nicely rounded. Probably burned it all
off, the way Luke did. She was like one of the china
figures in what they called over here the drawin' room,

the ones he had to handle so carefully when he dusted, but he was willin' to bet she'd bounce if you dropped her. He smiled as he watched her demolish a second muffin. Yes. This one, he surmised hopefully, would do.

"More?" he asked.

"Well . . . maybe just one more . . . They are the best muffins I've ever tasted."

"I wouldn't be surprised," Henry agreed, with the supreme confidence of One Who Knew.

Fiona was finishing off her second cup of coffee when the louvre doors to the kitchen swung inward and a man who could only be Charlie Whitesky came through them. Her hand froze in the act of raising her cup to her mouth. He was Rock Hudson in *Broken Arrow*, only more so. Never in her life – well, maybe once – had she seen a man so heroically handsome. At least six feet four inches and built to scale, he was a pale-copper Apollo with thick, shiny, coal-black hair and eyes to match. They focused on Fiona, snapped the shutter and wound on the film. "Hi!" he said, in a voice wrapped in black velvet. "You must be Fiona. Luke told me about you last night when I called. I'm Charlie Whitesky."

In a state of shock, Fiona took the proffered hand. He was absolutely electrifying. Totally male, physically overwhelming, a sensualist's dream. When he drew up the stool next to hers she could feel him like a four-bar electric fire. She gulped coffee. Did I say "interesting"? she asked herself dazedly. How in God's name am I ever going to get any work done around *him*?

She could feel his eyes on her, and was glad she had worn the amethyst suit again because she knew it flattered her skin, hair and eyes. Turning, she looked into his and was lost.

"Sioux?" she blundered, unable to think straight.

"Cheyenne on my mother's side."

"Oh . . ." Delight filled her with radiance. "A Human Being! Two Moons and Dull Knife . . ." She made a cutting motion with her hand.

The obsidian eyes showed surprise but his smile went to her head like the bubbles in a glass of champagne. "You know about Native Americans?"

"Some . . . I've read a lot, but I hope to learn more."

Fiona couldn't believe her luck. *Charlie Whitesky was a Cheyenne* – on his mother's side, anyway. Her favourite of all the tribes. The proudest of warriors, all organised into societies. Why, even the slang name for the American GI – dog soldiers – came from the Cheyenne warrior society of that name. This, Fiona thought dazedly, was just too much.

Charlie took the cup of coffee Henry placed in front of him.

"Thought you wasn't due back till tonight," Henry said.

"Got through my business quicker than expected, and when I called to tell Kemo Sabe he told me to haul ass, so here I am. Where is he anyway?"

"He had a late night."

"What else is new? He'd better make tracks, though. We have an eyes-only meeting at ten thirty."

"Anything I can do?" Fiona offered hopefully.

Charlie Whitesky turned his molten gaze her way. "Take it easy. You'll be on the grid soon enough."

18

If you're in the driver's seat, I can't wait, Fiona thought.

"Just stay loose, is all," Henry advised tolerantly.

Loose! was Fiona's reaction. I'm already in pieces!

Just then, shrugging into his jacket – he was conventionally dressed in a dark grey suit this morning – Luke pushed through the swing doors. He might have had a late night but he was bright-eyed and bushy-tailed. Obviously he had vast stores of energy.

"Morning." He flashed her a smile. "I see you've made yourself at home."

"Thanks to Henry and Mr Whitesky."

"Charlie . . ." corrected the owner of that name softly. Luke's eyes flickered briefly to where Charlie was finishing his coffee, but he spoke to Fiona. "I've left a report on your desk. Six copies and I need it for four o'clock this afternoon. I wrote it in the course of a bumpy plane ride so I hope you can decipher my writing. If not, ask Henry." He emptied the cup Henry handed him in two gulps. "Ready?" he asked Charlie.

"And waiting."

"Let's hit the trail, then."

Charlie rose to his overwhelming height. "*Washte*," he answered with mock solemnity. Once more he opened the oven door of his smile on Fiona, then they were both gone.

She let out a shaky breath.

"Yeah . . ." Henry, whose sleepy brown eyes missed nothing, said. "Ain't he, though."

Fiona hesitated, then plunged. "He said he was Cheyenne on his mother's side . . ."

Henry understood her at once. "His father was French-Canadian. His real name's Charles Dufresne, but after his father skipped and his mother married again – to a Northern Cheyenne – he took his stepfather's name."

Henry's voice was neutral, but Fiona, whose perception bordered on the fey, detected deeps where she'd need oxygen should she venture to explore them, so she did not do so. It was enough that she was already feeling out of her depth.

The report, scrawled on lined foolscap in a hand that was as rapid as the rest of him, made a pile an inch thick, and it had graphs and figures in it. Nor did he use punctuation so much as slashes, though when she read it through she found it to be precise in its details and easily assimilated. An underlined note at the top of the first page said, "American spelling, please." The shelf behind her desk carried several reference books as well as technical manuals, and there was a thick Webster's Dictionary.

Right, Fiona said to herself. Ss for Cs and no Us after Os. And concentrate. You can think about Charlie in your own time . . .

She was familiar with the word processing package, and was making rapid progress when Henry put his head round the door. "You want anythin', you holler, OK?"

"I will," she promised, aware that in Henry she had found a friend.

She was totally absorbed when he came in again, and this time he had a tray bearing a cup of coffee and a two-inch-thick piece of fudge brownie.

"I just now took one to Sleepin' Beauty, so you may as

well profit. I always let them sleep till eleven, then I got
my cleanin' to do."

The coffee was perfect and the brownie melted on the
tongue. If this morning's sample of the food in this house
was anything to go by, Penny had been right when she'd
said Henry was a menace to any woman trying to keep
her figure.

Some time later someone put a head round the open
door. "Luke?"

Fiona looked up. It was a blue-eyed, curvaceous
blonde in a strapless, clinging, sapphire-blue satin dress,
a feathered wrap hanging from the scarlet-tipped fingers
of one hand.

"Long gone," she advised pleasantly.

"Oh." The blonde pouted, tossing her long hair over
her shoulder as Henry materialised behind her.

"Taxi's waitin'," he announced.

"Oh," said the blonde again, this time with surprise.

"Downstairs," prodded Henry.

"Oh, well . . ." She shrugged. "Bye . . ." she trilled,
and was gone.

So that was an example of the harem, Fiona thought.
Very lovely. Very young. Very available. And none of my
business. But as she resumed her work she found herself
wondering what kind of woman attracted Charlie Whitesky . . .

At one o'clock, she was checking the first printed copy
when Henry appeared again.

"I got a nice little filet and a green salad with ranch
dressing. You interested?"

"Deeply."

"I'll bring you a tray."

"Can't I eat in the kitchen and talk to you?"

Obviously gratified: "Come ahead."

A good morning's work, Fiona thought on a satisfied smile as she swiftly made the corrections to the computer pages before setting the printer to run off the necessarily perfect copies.

Henry had opened a bottle of Californian Cabernet Sauvignon, and the steak he set before her parted at the mere threat of the knife, while the salad was crisp romaine lettuce, watercress, chicory, endive and avocado, all coated in the creamy ranch dressing.

"Henry, you are a magician," sighed Fiona as she put her knife and fork together on her empty plate.

"I been most other things, so why not?"

"What part of the South are you from?"

"How do you know I am?"

"I've been to most of the Southern states and I recognise the accent, even if I can't yet say whether it's from Alabama or Arkansas."

"I'm from Biloxi, Mississippi."

"And have you been with Mr Lucas for long?"

"We're Americans so we use first names around here, and I been with Luke for ten years. I was tendin' bar in Tulsa, and there was a fight one night when some Southern gents tried to show me a little of their good ol' Southern hospitality. He broke it – and them – up, and after I applied a little first aid I made him a pick-me-up. He said anyone as could perform such miracles was not to be let go. We been together ever since."

"You're very fond of him, aren't you?"

"He's the best." It was a statement of fact which brooked no contradiction.

"You must have seen a great deal of the world together."

"You name it and I reckon I seen it, but I'll still settle for the good old US of A."

"Homesick?"

"Home-lovin'. Want some apple pie à la mode?"

"Do I?"

The pastry was as crisp and light as the air trapped in it, while the apples were juicy and tart. "Where did you learn to cook like this, Henry?"

"I guess I just picked it up as I went along. I was a short-order cook once. I been a lot of things in my time."

"Including a boxer?"

Henry laid a finger against his broken nose. "How'd you guess?"

"And what is your impression of England?"

"It sure does rain a lot."

"That's why it's so green."

"That figures," Henry agreed. "More pie?"

"I couldn't. I have no more room for so much as a mouthful."

"Well, we don't usually eat dinner till eight so you got time to get your appetite back."

"Are we entertaining tonight?"

"Nope. Got to get you broke in easy."

She was collating the copies of the report ready for the binding machine when Luke returned. He flicked rapidly through the copy she handed him. He read fast too. "Fine

. . . Get them into their binders so I can give the clients their copies. You'll sit in and take notes. Any calls?"

She gave him a sheaf of meticulously noted messages: caller, time, response given. Some he frowned over, some he crumpled and threw away, others he gave back to her to note in the big, leather-bound desk diary it was one of her jobs to keep, as well as another labelled "The Where-abouts Book". Wherever Luke, Charlie or Fiona went outside the office, their destination, plus telephone number, had to be put in the book so they could be contacted at a moment's notice should it be necessary.

Charlie came in, throwing a smile at Fiona as he went to the door behind which the huge steel filing cabinet was kept, always locked. For such a big man he was all grace and lightness, yet she also got the impression of deliberation and control. She had to bring her attention quickly back to Luke when he asked: "Henry looking after you?"

"Like a den mother."

He grinned. "That means he's sworn you in as a member of the pack. Got your book? I want you to send an e-mail before the meeting."

The clients were of Middle Eastern origin: Lebanese, or perhaps Syrian. Fiona sat behind them, facing Luke so she could read his subtle signals, which he had arranged before the meeting. Watching him at work revealed another facet of what she was beginning to realise was a complex personality. He was the master of his subject, and thus able to answer all the tricky questions put to him. Charlie worked on the contract angle and handled its complications with the ease of one who knew only too well how to write a clause so as to be foolproof in any court of law. The two of them worked the four clients with the fluidity of a professional magic act, and Fiona was not in the least surprised when, at six o'clock, hands were shaken on a deal. As Luke saw them out she went to put her notes on disk, and while she was at it she printed out the standard form of contract she had discovered when exploring her computer's files. When Luke saw it he commented: "You a mind reader too?"

"I leave that to you and Charlie, but I have learned to anticipate."

"That can take the fun out of things." J. J. Lucas, she was learning, was a tease. "Right; I'll amend the contract – I expect you've already found Charlie's cache of subsidiary clauses – and once it's on file that file is locked and can be opened only when the right password is given. You, me, Charlie and Henry are the only ones who know it, and we change it every now and then. There's guys would give Fort Knox to get into my files so you memorise the password then forget it, OK?"

Fiona met the laser-beam eyes. "Yessir!" she snapped smartly.

Fiona could have sworn his mouth twitched, but he said only: "I'll be out to dinner. I usually am unless we're entertaining clients. Charlie will be here, though, and Henry, so you won't lack for company – unless you want to go out yourself, of course. Just tell Henry if you do and leave your whereabouts. Right, before I leave let's get the report of that meeting on file."

He didn't stand still while he dictated. He paced, or he peered out of the window, or he fiddled with something on the desk. It was not that he didn't know what he wanted to say; it was that he was a power-house of nervous energy fuelled by one hundred per cent octane vitality. Where Charlie was all grace and fluidity, Luke was all angles and sharp corners. And yet he was the one with the thousand and one fly-by-nights. She wondered if tonight's blonde would be a fresh one. With so much energy he must wear them out quickly . . .

When he left she went back to her desk. It was just on seven when Charlie materialised in his silent way, carrying two clinking glassfuls.

"Don't tell me," smiled Fiona. "You're a medicine man."

"This sort of medicine, yes. You've done well today. It was a New Girl's Handicap yet you still managed to win by a head. I think we've found Luke's match at last."

"Thank you." Fiona found she was deeply pleased.

"You are one very efficient lady." Pause. "Very pretty too."

Fiona gulped gin and tonic to cool her sudden heat before deflecting him with: "Where are you from, Charlie? You don't sound like Luke."

"That's because I was born in Colorado. He's from Oklahoma."

"Have you known him long?"

"Long enough."

It was easily said, and with a smile, but Fiona's well-honed perception detected the withdrawal, so she did not pursue the topic, asking instead: "Can you tell me something I've always wanted to have confirmed. Does the name 'Cheyenne' come from 'Sha-ha-na'? And what does that mean? And why did you call yourselves the Human Beings? I've got so many questions . . . Books are all very well, but there's nothing like talking to someone who can tell you how it really is."

Ten minutes later, when Luke put his head round the door to tell them he was off, neither of them saw or heard him. They were too deep in conversation – and each other. Both were unaware of the way his expression tightened or the clear eyes darkened, while the abrupt *snap* of the door went unheard.

Three

A pattern formed itself over the next weeks. Luke did indeed work like a demon, but it was as though something drove him, and either he had no idea how to turn off the engine or he was afraid that, if he did, he would find himself in the middle of nowhere. He was always ready to move at a moment's notice. Fiona soon learned to keep a bag packed and ready just in case, never knowing when he would put the phone down and say: "Right! Get the three of us on the first plane to Riyadh" (or Singapore, or Caracas or wherever), but she came to know what to expect when she got there: spending her time in a hotel suite with her laptop for company, when she wasn't sitting in on a meeting taking notes. But she always took an evening dress: something in silk jersey that wouldn't crease, since she never knew when they would be entertaining prospective clients to dinner.

In no time she found herself totally involved, and loving it. As a quick learner, it did not take her long to discover how Luke's mind worked, since hers worked in a similar manner. Within six weeks their relationship had reached the stage where he was relying on her utterly and trusting her implicitly, keeping nothing back from her where his work was concerned. With Henry, too, she formed a close working relationship, and once he discovered she was an old hand at what he called "high-class entertainin'", they worked in tandem to allow Luke to wine and dine a series of potentially valuable clients, not to mention visiting firemen: bankers, industrialists, money-men, wheeler-dealers. Fiona Sutherland was soon known as J. J. Lucas's right (some said left too) hand.

He knew an awful lot of people – there was always a raft of visiting Americans around the house – but Fiona soon realised that though he and Charlie worked closely together – they were partners, after all – the two men themselves were not friends. There was an undefined no man's land between them, one she sensed was strewn with mines. It was not enough to worry her, but she was always conscious of it, so she took care to give it a wide berth. Luke rang regular changes on his blondes, and since it was a part of his life he kept private she had no idea where he took them. She never saw Charlie with any woman. When he went out in the evening he went alone, and he came back the same way, but gradually, as Fiona became part of the set-up, he took to dining in with her, watching television perhaps, or just talking, and in no time at all Fiona was hooked, gaffed and in the basket. Charie Whitesky was a dish. He was also very clever highly intelligent and smooth as the very best butter. When after they got to know and were comfortably at ease with each other, he asked her to show him London, and she was only too pleased. Any time spent with Charlie was a bonus. She took him to see the tourist sights, and to some places tourists never got to see, courtesy of "some people I know", she told him vaguely. He enjoyed everything, and his looks earned Fiona envious stares from other women. When he turned out to be a marvellous dancer she was out for the count. She loved dancing, and Charlie's grace and lightness of foot made him a partner to die for.

One night it was late – almost 3 a.m. – when they got back, Fiona toting the magnum of Krug they had won at the charity ball she had taken him to.

"Nightcap?" asked Charlie.

"I'm already floating, but perhaps a cup of good American coffee . . ."

"Coming right up, after I put this champagne on ice for later."

"I'll be right with you . . ."

But when she switched on the lights in the living room, there was Luke, sprawled in one of the big suede chairs, black tie loosened, dinner jacket undone, and dead drunk.

"Where the hell have you been?"

Fiona flinched at his snarl. "Dancing."

"You're supposed to be here when I want you."

"You weren't here when I went out!"

"I'm here now. I told you: you're on call twenty four hours a day. What the hell do you think I pay you so much for? Lip service?"

Angry now, at both his tone and his attitude, Fiona proceeded to demonstrate her own. "Since when have you ever been here after eight o'clock on any night, unless you were entertaining clients?"

She was about to say more, when she felt a warning

hand on her arm. It was Charlie. "What's up, Kemo Sabe?" he asked lightly, but with an underlying something in his voice which made Fiona regard him with a frown. "Been stood up?"

Luke's ice-cube eyes were hot with hatred as he glared at Charlie. "You too! You're supposed to be here when I want you!" He was flushed, ugly drunk, spoiling for a fight. "You look very pleased with yourselves," he flung at them.

"Not without reason. We won a magnum of champagne in a raffle at the Grosvenor House charity ball."

"On *my* time!"

"You were out when we left."

Fiona was silent, utterly at a loss to understand this alarming, even frightening stranger. This was not the Luke she had thought she knew. But evidently Charlie did, because his hand on her arm had her turning towards him. His look was at once reassuring and an instruction. Fiona found herself saying obediently, "I'm going to bed," but as she turned to leave, Charlie's hand restrained her once more. Turning, she looked up at him enquiringly, whereupon he bent down from his great height and, drawing her to him, kissed her, devastatingly and at some length. When he released her, Fiona could only stand there, not seeing him but feeling him down to her very toenails. Swallowing hard: "Good-night," she managed to croak, before she fled, aware that Luke had watched it all.

Safe in her room, she fell on to her bed and tried to make sense of it all. Apart from being totally demolished by Charlie's kiss, she was a jumble of confusion because of Luke. What went on here? What sort of buried darknesses lay around, like pits to be fallen into? All of a sudden what had been no more than an exciting if demanding job had turned into a war, and in spite of all her map-reading she had still landed herself in the middle of the minefield she had determined to avoid. What had possessed Charlie to kiss her – for the first time – tonight of all nights, and in front of Luke? He had never laid so much as a respectful finger on her before, however much she might have longed for him to do so. Charlie White-sky, she had soon realised, could lead any woman down his garden path, no matter if it was paved with good intentions, high hopes or sweet dreams, yet until tonight he had always stuck to the well-lit main road. She had been the one to eye the shadowy culs-de-sac and dimly lit turn-offs. Now here she was at the bottom of his garden, in the newly dug section marked "Bedding Plants", presciently aware, with hollow disappointment, that she had been placed there deliberately. For some un-fathomable reason Charlie had flourished her at Luke, implying more – much more – than there presently was to their relationship. Why? And why was Luke drunk? Not bored drunk, or angry drunk, but vicious, tormented, *unhappy* drunk? What was he trying to drown?

Fiona shivered. In the space of minutes a familiar situation had changed to territory she did not recognise. And she had no idea why.

Damn! she thought resentfully. If those two have some kind of grudge match in progress then they can damn well fight it on their own. They're not going to use me as their whipping boy!

Next morning, Sunday, only Henry was in the kitchen when Fiona went downstairs, somewhat hesitantly because she had no idea what to expect, or from whom. Henry nodded when she wished him good-morning, but she sensed he was not in the mood for conversation. Even so, she wanted to know how the land lay.

"Where is everybody?" she asked brightly.

"Gone to take a little exercise. Handball. Luke and Charlie like to keep in shape."

Handball! thought Fiona. I would have thought a little hand-to-hand combat more in line with last night's feelings. But she demolished her breakfast – waffles with chokecherry syrup and whipped cream – then took a cup of coffee and the Sunday papers to her office. She was up to date with her work, and she had no idea when – or if – the two men would be back, so she decided to relax. Looking out of the windows, she saw a child throwing a ball for a dog to run and catch. That's me, she thought gloomily. Ready to run after Charlie's ball any time. As she stood there, she saw the bright red Camera come round the corner.

She was at her desk with the *Sunday Times* financial section open when she heard her door open. It was Luke.

"Hi!" he greeted her cheerfully.

"Good-morning," Fiona answered neutrally.

"That it is!" He was his usual crisp, brisk self. No sign of the mean streak of the night before. Or a hangover. It was as though it had never been. Perhaps he was one of those people who never remembered afterwards what they had done when they tied one on.

"You had breakfast?"

34

"Yes, thank you."

"Good. We're having a day off today. I think we need one."

You mean *you* do, thought Fiona.

"I thought we'd go for a drive, into the country maybe, have a pub lunch somewhere. You can take us someplace worth seeing."

Fiona was confounded, but, "Whatever you say," she answered dutifully.

They went in the Camera, the sports car which Luke had recently shipped over from America. It was a big car for a two-seater, but Fiona still had to shoehorn herself in between the two men. The filling in the sandwich? she wondered. Charlie laid his arm along the back of the seat, ostensibly giving Fiona more room, but resting his fingers negligently on her shoulder. Oh, yes, she was the filling in the sandwich, all right. Well, she would show them what a good dollop of Scots sauce could add to it!

They drove along the river and into the Thames Valley, through all the lovely little villages lining its banks. It was a tight squeeze: Charlie was big all round and Luke's endless legs took up all the available space. She was acutely conscious of the closeness of two male bodies: the pressure of arms, the brush of hands on her knees when Luke changed gear, for he drove as fast as he did everything else. But she was also conscious of something else even more disturbing. Charlie was flaunting her at Luke as the other half of a couple, saying, "We did this" and "We saw that" in a way which exaggerated what had really happened. Why? She could find no answer to that question yet, but of one thing she was becoming sure: Charlie had an ulterior motive. That he was devious she had already learned, but what was his game-plan here? Why was he so keen to establish them in Luke's eyes as a twosome? Luke had never asked her out, never once indicated that he saw her as anything else but an invaluable employee. So what difference did it make if she and Charlie became something more? Did he frown on intimate relationships between the people who worked with and for him? If so, he had never given any indication. So why was Charlie needling him? Obviously, she decided, there were things here she did not know.

They stopped for lunch at Bray: young English lamb roasted with rosemary and garlic and served with red-currant sauce, tiny new potatoes and mange-touts, followed by a luscious pudding which Fiona told the men was called Eton mess, thick with raspberries and fresh cream.

Afterwards she took them to Windsor, and, standing on the terrace of the castle, she pointed out the spires of Eton College.

"So that's where you won all your battles," Charlie mocked.

"Not all the ones we fought with you."

"Do I detect a note of relief?"

"America is what it is today because it won its independence," Fiona told him seriously.

"Now that", he responded gravely, "is taking pro-Americanism to its limit."

"I am pro-American. I thought I'd made that plain enough."

"Nothing about you is plain."

Luke turned from where he had been gazing into the distance. "Let's move on," he ordered.

As they got back into the car, he said to Charlie, "Your turn to drive." And this time it was his arm that stretched along the leather seat.

There's some kind of deadly game being played here, Fiona decided, and for some unknown reason I'm the prize: sandwiched – literally and metaphorically – between two men, one of whom is using me to get at the other. And just what is this particular game they're playing anyway? It's not one I've ever played.

She must have been frowning because she came out of her abstraction to hear Luke saying: "I'd offer you a penny for them but you look like they're priceless."

"Weight in gold," Fiona responded lightly. Then: "This dinner tonight. I remember you saying the guests are VIPs. What's my agenda?"

"They need cosseting, playing along."

"Motherly or womanly?"

"They have mothers of their own," Charlie said. "Just give them a liberal helping of that English cool: you know, there, but not *there*, if you know what I mean."

"Is that how you see us?"

"That's how you are. You look down on us colonial hicks from great height."

"Never!" Fiona exclaimed.

"Well, maybe not you in particular, but with the British the implication of superiority is always there."

"I had no idea we gave that impression."

"Stick around and that's not all you'll learn." There

was an inflexion in Charlie's voice which made Luke react with a sudden tensing of his long, lean length. Cool it! she thought rapidly before saying: "You mean earn while you learn?" in her best Edith-Evans-as-Lady-Bracknell manner.

Charlie laughed. "That's exactly what I mean," he agreed. "It's a combination of diction and accent. English as she is really spoke is the greatest put-downer in the world. No wonder you provide its greatest actors. That cut-glass accent is spellbinding – like your voice."

"Come on, put your foot down, Charlie," snapped Luke. "Time's a-wasting."

That evening Fiona went to check the dining table, putting the finishing touches to the flowers she had arranged for it: a mass of tightly budded Pinnocchio roses, the colour of her dress. She had flanked them with twin six-candle candelabras, finely carved in rock crystal to match the Baccarat glasses and the blades of the heavy silver cutlery with its ormulu handles. Henry had got out the best Rockingham china, and he was cooking up a storm in the kitchen. The clients represented a very great deal of money, and they were bringing their wives with them. Fiona had gone to town on her on appearance, knowing that wives meant they were being given the serious once-over.

Her dress was not new – several years old, in fact – but it was a favourite, a Zandra Rhodes, one of her full-skirted drifts of pure silk chiffon shading from deepest old rose to palest pink. Against her hair, glowing like the wine Henry would serve, and her fine, translucent skin, it looked fabulous. She had put her twenty-first-birthday pearls in her ears and round her throat, before misting herself with Patou's Joy. She fitted, she thought, checking her reflection in the Chippendale mirror on the far wall, Charlie's specification to the letter. A woman but also, very definitely, a lady.

Charlie thought so too, because when he entered the dining room, obviously looking for her, he stopped dead before saying, in a voice that curled her toes: "Oh, yes, yes indeed! They may have the money but there are still some things no amount of that will ever be able to buy!"

Fiona eyed him unsmilingly, ruthlessly suppressing the effect his own magnificence was having on her, in a flawlessly cut dinner jacket and a whiter-than-white shirt. Charlie was a peacock man. Always beautifully and expensively presented, he kept his window dressed at all times. Luke, on the other hand, wore clothes only because if he hadn't he would have been arrested for indecent exposure.

Now Charlie came over to where Fiona stood by the table, and she noticed his black tie was hanging loose. "I never could get the hang of these things," he said plaintively. "Us Native Americans are new to dudin' up like this."

Fiona's look demolished that for the fiction it was. "Pull the other one, it's got Big Ben on it." But as she reached up to tie the bow: "Don't go all breech-clouted brave on me, Charlie. Native Americans haven't worn them for almost a century. What I do want to know, though, is just what you are up to with Luke? You two are engaged in some kind of sudden-death play-off and I find myself an unwitting – and unwilling – participant. I don't like it and I warn you, if you're trying to involve me in the war between you two, I will not be drafted. I only work here. Remember that!" She patted the bow into place and stepped back.

"Too late . . . you fitted into the place that was waiting for you, and only you."

"Easy on the sugar, Charlie. Whatever situation existed before I came on the scene is none of my business, but I would appreciate you throwing some light on it before I trip and break my neck."

"Not with me around to catch you." His hands came up to circle her waist, draw her to him.

"I'm not fooling, Charlie!"

"Neither am I," he answered, and kissed her.

When she came up for air she made herself step back from him, reaching for a chair-back to prop up her shaky legs. As she did so she caught sight of herself in the big mirror, but what she stared into were were the ice-cube eyes of Luke, standing behind her in the open doorway. She moved her eyes to Charlie, and only just caught an expression that threw a bucket of cold water on the fire he had lit. He had known Luke was there! That was why he had kissed her. She levelled a look at him that bored a hole right between his eyes.

"There you are, Charlie," she said in a deadly voice. "I hope you're satisfied."

His smile said he was, but, "Perfectly," he confirmed.

Fiona turned to Luke, cucumber cool outside, hurting

furiously inside. "Is there anything I can do for you?" she asked.

He shook his head. "You look very nice," he said politely.

"Thank you. If you'd like to check the table . . . I've put the minister here, next to me; you're at the other end with the minister's wife on your right . . ."

"I'm sure it's all as Charlie says – perfect," he said.

Fiona could take no more. "Then if you'll excuse me I'll just go and check with Henry as to how his preparations are coming along."

Henry took one look at her face and reached into his private cupboard for the bottle of Jack Daniels he kept there.

"Sit a spell," he said. "Everythin' is under control. They ain't goin' to eat *you*."

I've already been carved up, Fiona thought bleakly, as she downed the finger of bourbon in one gulp. She felt bruised and used. Even as she had warned Charlie not to use her he had done so. How sure he must be of his hold on her to be able to act so confidently. Hold? she thought derisively. Arm-lock more like.

"Ain't no harm in a little liquid courage," Henry was saying. "Just because this is a big one don't say there won't be a bigger one along later."

There won't be a bigger one than me, Fiona thought bitterly. Fool, that is.

"I ain't got no worries," Henry continued. "Luke's the best there is. What he don't know about the business he's in ain't worth knowin'."

Neither is Charlie, Fiona thought on a pang. He is bad

medicine. Taken even once a day, he's poison. He could be the death of you, Fiona. Kick the habit before he kicks you in the teeth.

Henry eyed her stiff white face. Something had her hangin' on the ropes, and five would get you ten thousand it was that son of a bitch Charlie Whitesky. He'd seen the way that smooth-talkin' fancy man had started homin' in on her. Bad news.

"Luke ain't worried none," he said deliberately. "He knows he can trust you to do your best. 'She's squared the triangle,' he said to me."

Fiona looked up from her glass.

"Ain't you noticed? All I get these days when I ask him anythin' is, 'Ask Fiona. She'll know.' He trusts you, and take it from me, he don't trust nobody he don't like." He paused, then struck home. "Charlie, now, he's different. He don't always mean what he says – or does, come to that. He's a great one for foolin' around – and foolin' people – but most of all, foolin' himself. Charlie is . . . all mixed up, and it's all to do with him bein' half Cheyenne and half French-Canadian. Oh, he's clever and educated but he's also mighty proud. Charlie may be mixed-blood, as they say, but he thinks and feels one hundred per cent Cheyenne, and Native Americans has long memories. Take it from me, Charlie has the longest memory I've ever known."

So Henry had noticed too. Enough to be so concerned as to issue a warning.

"You go and lay 'em in the aisles," he encouraged. "Tell the truth, you look good enough to eat, but I reckon my dinner will do just as well."

Fiona reached out to squeeze his hand. "What would I do without you?" she asked rhetorically, just as the doorbell chimed.

At just after twelve thirty Henry shut the door on the last of the departing guests, and Fiona dropped back into a big chair with a relieved sigh. It had been hard work but in the end a triumph. The minister had been charming – and charmed – while his wife, dazzlingly beautiful and wreathed in emeralds, had been vastly taken with Charlie, who skilfully used the advantage it gave. The minister's English had been halting, but he and Fiona had conducted their conversation in French, she acting as interpreter for him with Luke, who now came to stand in front of her, pulling his black tie loose.

"You did a great job. Thanks."

"My pleasure."

Charlie came up behind Luke. "Now I know how come you British conquered the world," he said. "You did us proud tonight."

He bent down to lift one of her hands to his mouth in a gesture of homage. Swiftly she snatched it back. "Why, Charlie . . . I thought you were part Cheyenne, not charlatan."

His eyes gleamed. "I've learned a lot since I left the reservation."

"Yes," she said pointedly. "So I've noticed. Now I will bid you both good-night."

In her room she sat down on the stool in front of her dressing table and stared at herself in its mirror. She was flushed, brilliant-eyed; her skin glowed and her hair took

43

fire from the light. The effect of two attractive men in competition over you, she told herself, but don't fool yourself, my girl. There's a hell of a lot more going on here than sexual rivalry. This is not just another battle in the endless war between the sexes – even if that is at present raging between you and Charlie. Trouble is, unless you stop it, you could lose the best job you've ever had. It's already begun to spoil it.

She had never liked these atmospheres, being both sensitive to and adversely affected by them, and there was one wreathing this household that threatened her well-being, not to mention her bank balance, for she had been salting away money at a fast clip for her projected year's sabbatical in the United States.

The best – the only – thing to do, she decided, was make it clear to Charlie that there was no way she would allow him to use her as a weapon in his war with Luke, whatever that war was about (and try as she might she could still not come up with so much as an idea). She only knew that it was personal, deeply and vindictively so, and that the aggressor was Charlie. Bitter experience as well as acute perception informed her of this. As a much younger woman – still a girl, in fact – another man had used her for his own ends. It had taken her months – years – to recover. There was no way she would go through that again. Because the next time it would be the death of her.

Four

Luke and Charlie were out all next day, which gave her plenty of time to prepare the contract Charlie had drafted and left ready for her to put on file. She was checking it carefully when she heard Luke say: "I thought *I* had a great capacity for work, but you go though it like a shredding machine!"

Fiona looked up at him. "That is what you pay me for," she told him, beginning as she meant to go on.

"Even so, I think a little something extra is called for after all you did last night. The minister complimented me on your – er – talents. I think he had a takeover in mind, but I told him you were already taken. This is just a little token of my appreciation." He dropped a small package in front of her. Probably perfume, she surmised, both surprised and touched. But when she tore off the wrapping it was not perfume but a flat jeweller's box with the discreet Asprey logo on it. Startled now, she looked back up at Luke to find he was watching her intently.

Turning back to the box, she pressed the little button and its lid flew up to reveal, nestling on a bed of white satin, an exquisitely jewelled rose, its petals of rose diamonds, its leaves and stalk of baguette emeralds.

45

Her jaw dropped. Totally robbed of breath, she stared up at him.

"You don't like it," he said flatly.

"Like it! *Like it!* Luke, it's the most exquisite thing I ever saw in my life, but I can't possibly accept it. I have done nothing that you should buy me something as costly as this. I—"

"You like roses, I know. You wear the colour and you always smell like one."

Totally taken aback by now, she spluttered: "But Luke, surely you must see that I can't—"

"But me no buts. Last night you helped me swing a very profitable deal and all I'm doing is showing my gratitude."

"But you already pay me well over the odds."

"So this is a bonus."

Fiona's fingers caressed the beautiful thing. It was gorgeous, but there was no way she could accept it. Not only because she had done nothing to deserve so rich a gift, but also because she could not rid herself of the suspicion that Luke was doing a Charlie. Oh God, she thought, despairingly. What have I gone and got myself into here?

"Just so long as you like it," Luke pursued.

"Oh, I do. It's beautiful, but I still can't accept it. It's not—"

"Done?"

"Well . . . no, it's not. Not between employer and employee."

"I thought we'd gone beyond that stage, or isn't my rating as high as Charlie's?"

"I make no distinction between you," Fiona said stiffly.

"You could have fooled me – except I wouldn't try that, if I were you. But feel free to fool yourself." Nodding at the jewel, "Wear it in good health," he added sardonically, before walking out.

Oh, damn, thought Fiona, putting her head in her hands. Damn and damn and damn!

That night, she went with Charlie to a long-arranged concert of American music at the Barbican. Copeland, Barber, Ives. But her mind was in such a febrile state that she was unable to quiet it, give it over to music she loved. All she could think of was the situation she was in, and how she could resolve it. Afterwards, they went for a late supper to a club where there was also a dance floor, but Fiona was so *distraite* that Charlie finally protested. "Fiona, I get the feeling that you're not only not out with me, you're out of reach."

Now! she thought, folding her hands together on the tabletop to stop them trembling. "If I am, it's because I have things on my mind, and since they concern you this is as good a time as any to tell you what they are. As they used to say in pre-politically correct days, 'honest Injun', Charlie. I want straight answers. Like why are you using me against Luke? You're stitching him up and using me as the needle – why?"

Charlie's sigh was theatrical. "My fault for preferring women with brains. I should be like him and stick to bodies only. They're a lot less trouble."

"What Luke does and with whom he does it is none of

my business. You are, because you are making me your business, and I want to know why. Just exactly what is it you want from me, Charlie?"

His smile was a slow burn. "I thought you'd never ask."

Fiona hung on grimly. "You're using me, aren't you?"

"Not in the way I'd like."

Angry now: "You know damned well what I'm talking about. You're using me to get at Luke."

"Hardly. You do that all by yourself."

"Only since you put the idea into his head. I am well aware that you have been . . . flourishing me at him. He thinks we have something going—"

"I'm doing my best," Charlie protested. "Let's dance and I'll prove it to you."

Before she could refuse he had grasped her wrists and was pulling her up from the table and on to the dance floor. "That music is far too good to waste."

As always, being in his arms, acutely and physically conscious of all that potent masculinity and grace, melted her down to a puddle. He fitted her close against him but even as she laid her face against his shirt she desperately went on trying: "It's no good, Charlie, you're bad medicine . . ."

"That's the kind as is supposed to do you most good."

Trying to be firm: "You are incorrigible."

"And you are incredible."

Fiona shook her head as though to clear it. "It's no use. You see, I'm not convinced that it's me you want. My feminine instinct keeps telling me that I am no more to you than a means to get at Luke. Why won't you be honest with me?"

He didn't answer at once, but looking up at him she could see he was staring over her head with an expression she had come to know but had never been able to read. Finally he said, "I thought you would be good for him; a change from the blondes."

Fiona drew back and flashed him a look that spoke volumes, complete with preface, footnotes and bibliography. "That won't wash. Altruism is most definitely *not* your style."

"OK, so I found out you'd be even better for me . . ."

Unwilling to believe him, or to look away from those obsidian eyes, Fiona said unsteadily: "I won't let you *count coup* on me, Charlie. I'm not something you can hang on your lodgepole."

"You know a lot about Native Americans, but you don't know everything," Charlie said, suddenly cold and implacable.

Fiona despaired. Every time she tried to call for an answer from him all she got was a wrong number. That banked-fires exterior of his concealed an interior that never melted, for at his heart was a resolve as cold as any Colorado winter, a resolve that mattered to him far more than she ever would – or could. In spite of his overwhelming physical attraction for her, she intuited that he was capable of inflicting enormous damage on her in pursuit of his aim – not physical damage, but the emotional kind, where the destruction was hardest to mend. If she let him take her to the heights, as she sensed he could, and then dropped her once she had fulfilled her purpose, she would fragment beyond repair. Yet in his arms, feeling his body against her, wanting him, knowing he wanted her, it was immeasurably difficult not to let him have his way. She had to fight through the swamping wave of his sensuality, clench her teeth so as not to say, "All right, Charlie, whatever, wherever ... I'm yours ..."

"We have to talk about this," she insisted doggedly.

"Talk never got us anywhere. Talk sold us down every river we crossed and not even so-called-sacred pieces of treaty paper helped us in the end."

Suddenly he was a stranger: no longer the urbane, smooth-as-silk Ivy League lawyer, but a man whose ancestors had worn breech-clouts, eagle feathers and necklaces of bones, not to mention human scalps. Was that what he was doing to Luke? Obtaining revenge for centuries of betrayal by the white men who had stolen everything, from not only the Cheyenne but the whole Indian nation? Oklahoma had a long history where Native Americans were concerned.

Her mind was a jumble of confusion as Charlie's powerful sensuality put all coherent thought to flight. As if he sensed it, he drew her closer to him. She felt his breathing change, deepen, and suddenly had a sharp sense of fright. But then, she realised in a flash of insight, she always had been afraid of him. It was that sense of danger which had attracted her in the first place. That and the fact that something drove him. She knew that once he started she would never be able to stop him. Even now, she was powerless against the sheer overwhelming physicality of him, the control she now felt straining at the leash.

As though he read the subtle shifts in her own body, he

raised his head to look down at her and they exchanged a long, deeply penetrating look, during which their relationship shifted, tilting so that the balance came down on his side.

Taking her by an unresisting arm, he walked her off the dance floor and back to their table, summoned the waiter, paid the bill, lifted her wrap from her chair and laid it over her shoulders before leading her helplessly away.

She got into the car blindly, in a state of time suspended, unable to do anything except follow obediently, never taking her eyes from that beautiful profile, chiselled bronze in the light of the streetlamps, his mouth firm and compressed – the mouth she wanted, more than anything, to claim with her own.

When at last he stopped the car (where, she had no idea, only that he did it in such a way as to indicate he shared her feelings), they fell into each other's arms as if by homing instinct.

Then there was a long silence, punctuated only by ragged breathing, small gasps, harsh intakes of breath, small rustles of clothing, and Fiona's blurred voice murmuring, "Charlie . . . Oh God, Charlie . . ." Whenever he lifted his mouth from hers to move it down her throat to her breasts, her hands were in the thick black hair so that she could bring his head back to her avid, responsive mouth, lost to everything but the feel of him, the taste of him, dizzied and dazzled by the way he kissed her: slowly, mind-bendingly, nakedly erotic. Yet even in the midst of her delirium, some still-rational, buried-deep-for-safety part of her sounded an alarm, and in an effort to apply the brakes she tore her mouth from his and buried her face in his shirt, trying to clear her befuddled mind. Under her cheek she could feel the hammer of his own heart, and when at last she raised her head to look at him her eyes were deep, dark pansies, the pupils enlarged and drugged-looking.

His own were hot and black. He was as aroused as she was. "You said something about being used . . ." he said in a thick voice.

Fiona felt a chill cool her heated body. "Not this kind of usage." She sat up, removing herself from him, physically and emotionally. "Just what am I to you, Charlie? A special woman or just the means to a special end? Don't use me that way." In spite of herself she knew she was pleading. "I wouldn't be able to cope with that."

"Around you I'm not always in control of my actions," Charlie murmured, bending his head to the V of her breasts, the touch of his tongue making her arch convulsively. "You have an incredible effect on a man . . . I could have done with you a long time ago . . ."

"Why? What happened then?"

He sat up and back, as though she had pressed a hidden spring. "You're a clever girl, Fiona Sutherland."

Again Fiona felt that prescient chill. "And you don't like that, do you?"

"I'm not used to it."

"But you *are* using me – aren't you? To get at Luke . . ." She sat up straighter, firming her resolve. "I won't—" She had been going to say "let you hurt Luke through me" but instinct made her change it to "play your game, Charlie."

His smile licked her like a hungry flame. "This is playing?"

"The way you see it, yes."

"I would never hurt you, Fiona." He sounded hurt himself.

Sadly, because yet again her instincts were telling her it was the truth: "Oh yes you would," she told him. "If it suited you."

He sat back and for a moment there was a silence before he put an end to it by picking up her hands and kissing them both in a gesture that was at once respectful and deeply admiring. "You're quite a girl," he complimented her sincerely. "Oh yes, quite a girl."

Then he started the car again and drove them home.

Fiona didn't sleep a wink that night. Apart from the physical clamour Charlie had aroused, only to leave unsatisfied, she was deeply troubled, full of fears and convinced she was not handling this right. Her emotions kept getting in the way of her judgement. The only thing in which she could find some kind of bitter satisfaction was that she knew beyond doubt she had encountered a man much too dangerous to be trusted. What she could not yet fathom was just what it was that made him so. She only knew it had to do with whatever grudge he held against Luke. But if he hated his partner that much, why be his partner in the first place? What tied them together? What kept them tied? That, she was convinced, was where the problem – if ever she could find what that *was* – lay.

The best – the only – thing to do, she resolved finally,

as the sky paled and the birds began their dawn chorus, was to withdraw from the situation. Become as impersonal as it was possible to be. Make it plain to both men that she only worked there – and temporarily. Anything personal was a no-no. And to prove it she would return the diamond rose to Luke.

She acted on her resolve that day – politely but firmly made it plain that she was not available for anything that did not involve what she was paid for: hard work. Luke gave her a searching look, and though he took back the rose without comment, she had the feeling that what she was doing suited him fine. Charlie said nothing, as was his way; he liked to keep you guessing. But she was aware he was not best pleased, probably because no woman had ever said no to him in his life. And while she did not particularly like the look of her face with her nose cut off, she did not see what else she could do.

One Thursday morning about a week later, Luke announced that he and Charlie would be flying out to the Gulf next day. "It's a base camp and no place for women, so you're on your own for the weekend. Take it off, you've been working hard lately. Leave your whereabouts in the book and take your cell-phone with you. OK?"

Fiona decided at once to go home. She felt the need to unwind – if she could, since Charlie had her tied with reef knots. So she called her mother, managed to get a seat on the midday plane and flew to Inverness not long after Luke and Charlie's private jet had taken off for the Gulf.

Her mother was waiting for her with the car.

"You look fagged," was her critical greeting after a

loving hug and kiss. "Working yourself to death as usual, I suppose?"

"It is a demanding job, Mummy. I told you, remember, but it pays top whack."

"You're still bent on this sabbatical of yours?"

"Absolutely."

Her mother, a more mature replica of her daughter down to the hair and eyes, sighed and said: "Stubborn as a mule. Just like your father."

She eyed Fiona's somewhat pale face with misgiving. She knew that hunted look in the eyes, the tautness to the mouth. A man, she thought, and obviously not doing it right this time either.

She herself, having been married for thirty-eight blissful years before her husband died, peacefully in his big leather chair by the fire, had hoped for the same kind of happiness for her daughter, but it had not turned out that way, since Fiona had put her emotions in cold storage and concentrated on what she could cope with: work. At thirty-two, Shona Sutherland had been married nine years and was the mother of three children. At the same age, Fiona lived alone. But now, with that same uncanny Celtic precognition her daughter had inherited, she knew that Fiona had met a man. And that he was trouble.

"There's just the two of us," she said, sliding her arm through Fiona's as they walked to the car. "Iain's in Edinburgh and, the last I heard, Hamish's ship was somewhere in the South Atlantic. So you can relax and let it all hang out, as I believe they say nowadays . . ."

And it was indeed relaxing to be able to wear a pair of

faded jeans and an old sweater; to walk the dogs for miles
along the lochside, over the hills and through the forests;
to startle the red grouse and send them streaking and
clucking over the heather, and catch a glimpse of a
majestic twelve-point on the distant skyline; to listen
to the sound of gulls, and smell and feel the very essence
of the Highlands of Scotland.

By the Sunday morning she felt all her creases had
been ironed out; she had slept long, eaten well and
manhandled London and her troubles to the back of
her mind.

After breakfast, she took the dogs out for a last long
walk. It was a damp late-October day, the air heather-
fragrant, the loch slate-coloured and sullen, the wind
bracing. She tramped for miles along the deserted lochside, unrecognisable as the soignée Fiona Sutherland.
The dogs – Rusty and Red, setters both – were in high
spirits, chasing each other into the water, splashing after
gulls and barking frenziedly at the occasional low-flying
grouse. It was a quarter to one when she came back over
the lawns, only to stop dead when she saw the big
American car parked on the gravel sweep in front of
the house.

Her first reaction was anger. God! she thought furiously. They think they own you! She had used the
whereabouts book as requested, brought along her
state-of-the-art cell-phone which meant she could be
reached from just about anywhere, and she hadn't heard
a word. Now here they were intruding into her private
life. That was the trouble with Americans. They thought
an introduction gave them squatters' rights.

He was in the library, sitting in her father's Georgian wing-chair, long legs stretched towards the bright flames of the peat-and-driftwood fire, listening to her mother chattering away in the opposite chair, but he was on his feet instantly Fiona entered, bending down to pat the dogs who bounded forward to sniff and investigate.

Fiona regarded him unsmilingly.

"You never told me you worked for an oil tycoon," her mother chided. To Luke: "I have to prise information out of her."

"My work is confidential, Mummy. You know that."

"My dear, if I worked for someone like Mr Lucas the whole would know about it."

Carefully, as if walking on eggs, Luke said: "I got through things quicker than expected in the Gulf, and as there was a lift on a plane coming to Aberdeen I thought I'd kill two birds with one stone, so to speak. There's an oil producers' conference there and I'll need you. Henry told me you were up here, so when I arrived at Dyce I called and your mother said to come right on over . . ."

"I thought he could join us for lunch," that lady said blithely, eyeing her daughter's face. So, she thought, this is not him. Still, one must deal with what one has . . .

"A glass of sherry, Mr Lucas?" she invited, stretching out a hand to the bell-pull.

"Luke, and yes please."

Putting on her glasses, Lady Sutherland saw Fiona that much more clearly and exclaimed: "Heavens, you're all damp. Go and have a hot bath before lunch – you've got time. Logie tells me it's a soufflé to start with, and they won't wait, but he hasn't put it in the oven yet . . ."

With another darkling look at Luke, Fiona stalked out.

"No doubt you already know that my daughter's bark is much worse than her bite," her mother consoled him.

"Well, her bite can draw blood . . ."

Amethyst eyes sparkling: "Do tell . . ."

Fiona soaked in hot, scented bubbles for fifteen minutes, then dressed in a well-cut pair of mole-grey velvet trousers and a paler cashmere sweater, tying back her hair with a grey velvet ribbon and leaving her face bare of make-up. She was off duty, after all. As she left the room the gong sounded.

After lunch, Lady Sutherland said to her: "Luke has never been in a Scottish castle before. Why not show him round? Tea at four thirty as usual, and if you go out again, put on coats. That mist can soak you through in half an hour."

Luke's heels rang on the flags of the hall, accompanied by the click of the dogs' nails as they padded after them.

"Nobody will believe me back home," he said, sounding disbelieving himself. "Me with a real Scottish chieftain's daughter for a PA. I should have realised that you did the manor-born bit so well because you were actually born in one. Why didn't you ever mention it?"

"Why should I?" Fiona asked with the surprise of one who had never had to do any such thing. "Just because I was born in a castle doesn't mean I'm too grand to work for a living. Besides, my private life has nothing to do with my working life and I have never used the one to promote the other."

He took the hint and turned it into a challenge. "You're mad I came, aren't you?"

"It is – still – my weekend off!"

"It was your mother invited me over. It's only a hundred miles or so. I'd do twice that much in a morning back home."

"Don't come the all-American with me, Luke. I'm not a client."

"Thank God for that! I'd have a hard time selling myself to you!"

Fiona was taken aback by the sudden hardness showing through the easygoing surface. The clear eyes were as cold as the ice with which he loaded his drinks, while the whipcord had been transmuted into steel. Under the façade of the hard-working, easygoing (as long as things were going his way), laconic cowboy was another man. She had seen him briefly the night he was drunk, but he was sober now. Nevertheless, Fiona was burning with the angry suspicion that he was trying to steal a march on Charlie.

"Where's Charlie?" she demanded.

"Still in the Gulf. Why? I thought you'd cut him off at the knees."

Fiona was so taken aback she was speechless.

"I have eyes," Luke went on.

Which have always seen a great deal more than I have given them credit for, she realised, even as her smile glimmered at the Americanism.

"What's so funny? he demanded suspiciously.

"The picture of Charlie cut off at the knees . . ."

His smile was slow but it soon turned to a grin. "Yeah . . ."

Unaccountably feeling less uptight, Fiona said: "Come on then, I'll give you the grand tour."

He was fascinated by everything, especially the armoury, which included her late father's collection of claymores.

"These are beautiful – if awful heavy. Now I see why the Scots are always referred to as brawny." He smoothed the length of lethal steel. "Not only beautiful but functional with it. Like you," he added.

Fiona turned away. "Now I'll show you the dungeons where we kept the prisoners taken in clan battles."

She heard him sigh. "Lead on, Macduff . . ."

Her glance was sharp but he met it blandly.

In the depths of the castle she demonstrated, with almost malicious relish, the uses of the thumbscrews, after which he examined with fascinated interest the names scratched into the foot-thick walls. "A McK – 1589," he read out loud, before whistling. "Wow! The Spaniards had just gotten a foothold on the coast of California back then; the rest of America belonged to Charlie's folks."

Fiona moved away. She needed no reminders of Charlie, thank you very much.

She led him up the spiral staircase again, this time right to the top and the walkway along the battlements, where she leaned out over the drop to the rocks along the edge of the loch, a hundred feet below. She felt Luke come to stand behind her.

"Fiona," he said, in the voice of a man who was risking his all, "throw me over if you like, but . . . what happened between you and Charlie?"

He took a step back as she swung round violently to face him. "What is it with you two? You don't trust each other an inch! Are you in competition or something? Because if you are, let me tell you here and now, I will not be be fought over like some juicy bone!"

"Charlie and I go way back—"

"That much is obvious, but to what? Between you, I have been placed in an untenable position and I don't like it. I am well aware that there are personal matters I am not privy to, but as I only work for you they are none of my concern. What I resent is being used as a pawn in whatever game you're playing."

"You're a smart girl, Fiona."

"Now you even *sound* like him!"

"Don't make the mistake of thinking I am in any way like him." It was a warning, but Fiona's anger was well alight by now.

"I made my mistake back at the beginning by agreeing to work for you. Now I've had enough. I will go with you to Aberdeen, but that ends it! Once we get back to London I'll find you a replacement. I'm well aware of what it is you need by now."

"Not possible. You are irreplaceable."

"Spare me the flattery, if you please."

"I'm not being flattering. I'm being truthful."

Which, since Luke never lied, was unanswerable.

"I don't want you to go, Fiona. We work together like two halves of a whole. You understand me, anticipate me, fit in so well because you were custom-made for the job. Nobody else will ever slot in so well."

"Then why are you both trying to shape me to some end only the two of you know about?"

"I haven't tried to do any such thing. I repeat: don't confuse me with Charlie."

"Really! Then why did you bother to come personally to collect me? You could have left a message. I could have joined you in Aberdeen tonight."

He didn't answer her straight away, and when he did it was obliquely. "I will admit Charlie and I have old scores to settle, but if I promise that you won't be involved in them in the future, will you change your mind?"

"*You* will promise, but what about Charlie?"

"Leave Charlie to me." The note in his voice made her skin prickle, but she was not about to give up so easily. "Why won't you take no for an answer?" she demanded irritably.

"Because it is not the answer I want."

It was a display of that same tenacity which made him such a good businessman.

"All right, I'll think about it," she lied. "Will that do?"

"No. But it will have to do for now."

She shivered suddenly. "Let's go and get warm. It's freezing up here."

Logie had made up the fire and it was a roaring blaze. The dogs were lying in front of it. "Friendly dogs," Luke commented, as they got up to greet him, feathered tails waving like fans.

"That chair was my father's. Rusty and Red were his dogs."

He glanced up at the portrait hanging above the massive stone fireplace: a man in the full fig of a Highland chieftain. Sir John Sutherland, ninth Baronet. "Is that him?"

"Very much so. As he was, there he is."

"But you look like your mother."

"My brothers look like Father – Sutherlands both. I'm more of a Fraser, my mother's clan."

"How many brothers?"

"Two. Iain, the eldest, manages the estate. He's in Edinburgh just now. Hamish, my younger brother, is in the Royal Navy."

"But you all have red hair?"

"Yes."

The grandfather clock in the corner by the big window chimed the half-hour and as it did so Lady Sutherland entered the room. "What, sitting in the dark? Switch on the lamps, darling. I'm dying for a cup of tea. Afternoon naps do that to one. Ah, Logie, right on time as usual . . ."

The butler's tray, laid for tea with kettle, teapot, spirit lamp and china, was set in front of her, the old-fashioned cake-stand, containing freshly toasted bannocks, scones, Dundee cake and shortbread, placed to her left. "The scones I can recommend, Luke, and the loganberry jam is of my own making. Now then, milk or lemon?"

They left for Aberdeen at six o'clock. "Gracious, what a monster!" exclaimed Lady Sutherland, eyeing the big Buick. "Makes my little Renault look positively squished."

She kissed and embraced her daughter. "Bye, darling. Ring me when you're safely back." Turning to Luke, she shook hands warmly. "Goodbye, Luke. Do come and see us when next you're in Scotland – with or without my daughter."

"I'd like that, ma'am."

She stood waving until they rounded the bend in the drive. "What a nice lady," Luke said. "Mothers come in all shapes and sizes but yours is custom-made, like you."

"What about your own?"

"She died when I was seven, my father three years ago. And I was an only child." The reason for his self-sufficiency? Fiona wondered. Then remembered the blondes.

The mist had turned to rain which, as they drove east, became heavy, and the sound it made thrumming on the roof of the car, along with the steady swish of the windscreen wipers, was somnolently soothing. Fiona snuggled into the fake-beaver collar of her coat and closed her eyes. Her long walk that morning and the ensuing emotional wrangle had tired her. Luke drove expertly, if fast, and in a silence that she appreciated since she was not in the mood for conversation. She was out of practice at handling her emotions. After losing badly at the game of hearts she had stuck to solitaire, a game one could play single-handed.

Luke had turned on the heater, and its warmth pushed her ever nearer to sleep. He wouldn't mind if she dozed off. He was an easy man to be with. Around him there was none of the dry-mouthed, heart-fluttering awareness Charlie provoked. Yet he was an attractive man in his lean, whipcord way. The blondes obviously thought so. They kept coming – and going. Charlie never got calls from any women. She had the feeling he kept his personal affairs wrapped in the same cloak of secrecy with which he covered everything that did not concern work. But then, he was as closed as Luke was open. She was never sure of what – if anything – Charlie was thinking or feeling. Luke she could for the most part read like a book – the large-print edition – except when it came to whatever it was that lay simmering between the two men. She moved restlessly. That was one groove she was determined not to get stuck in.

Luke glanced across at her. She was on the verge of sleep, her face framed in the collar of her coat: somewhat pale, lashes thick and dark on her cheek, mouth parted slightly. Damn you, Charlie, he swore darkly. This is one game I can't let you win, because if I do I'll lose a hell of a lot more than even you realise . . . and that's something else I'm not about to let you know either . . .

Five

Fiona became aware that someone was saying her name, but she only muttered crossly and burrowed back into the pillow.

"Hey, sleepyhead, wake up. We're almost there." It was Luke, and he had a laugh in his voice.

"Almost where?"

"Aberdeen. We'll be at the hotel in less than five minutes."

She yawned, opened her eyes, then closed them again as lights dazzled her, squirming deeper into the pillow until she realised that it was no pillow but Luke's shoulder. She sat up at once. "Heavens! Have I slept all the way?"

"Every mile, and had pleasant dreams, from the smile on your face."

"I don't remember," she lied. She had been dreaming of Charlie.

"If you want to you can go straight to bed when we get to the hotel. You have your own suite. I've stayed there before. They know me."

Which was no understatement, for even as they entered the foyer he was hailed, back-slapped, hand-shaken and even bear-hugged by men wearing stetsons and the

kind of jackets Fiona associated with JR in *Dallas*. She
was not the only woman, but the others were of the kind
whose long, manicured and obviously silicone nails had
never tapped a keyboard in their lives.

"How about some dinner?" Luke asked.

"Not for me, thank you. You go ahead. I shall have an
early night so as to be bright and smiling in the morning."

"Sure?"

"Positive. Just hand me my key . . ."

"OK. Conference starts at ten o'clock sharp."

"I'll be there."

Her suite had a large sitting room with all the usual
amenities and then some, including a bar, a fridge, a large
vase of fresh flowers, a cellophane-wrapped basket of
fresh fruit and a bottle of a decent champagne on ice. She
ignored them all and was in bed within twenty minutes
and asleep in another five, but early in the morning – 2
a.m. by her clock radio – she was awakened by the sound
of general merriment in the corridor: a group of men and
women. One was Luke – she would know that laugh
anywhere – and she was willing to bet one of the women
was a blonde. Turning over, she went back to sleep.

The conference next day lasted until 4 p.m., after
which Luke dictated notes. He then went into huddles
with various groups while she went upstairs to her laptop. At seven thirty they met in the bar, where she was
introduced to so many people that even her excellent
memory had trouble remembering all the names, until,
refusing all offers of dinner, Luke bore her off to a table
for two in a quiet corner.

"You don't have to desert all your friends because of me, you know," Fiona protested.

"Don't be fooled by all the back-slapping. In this business there's always a knife up the sleeve. And I've been with them all day in one way and another. A nice quiet dinner is what I need right now. The food is good here, by the way. Henry's word."

"In that case . . ." She ordered smoked salmon, followed by roast haunch of venison – "I was brought up on both." Luke said that sounded great and had the same.

While he consulted the wine list Fiona looked round the crowded room. "A full house, but then, oil is a competitive business."

"Has to be. The reserves won't last for ever – that's why there's such a scramble to come up with new fields all the time."

"How did you get into it?"

"My great-great-grandfather was a former professional soldier, a captain in the Union Army who lost an arm at Chancellorsville. When he left the Army, he was a young man of twenty-four and he headed west. By 1889 he was a store owner in Denver when he heard there was to be a great land-grab in what was known as Indian territory: land that had been taken away by the United States government from the Five Civilised Tribes of Oklahoma because they'd fought for the Confederacy. He decided that if there was land to be grabbed he'd do his damnedest to grab as much as he could, because he was married by then and the father of three, besides which he'd always wanted to establish a cattle ranch but never could afford to buy the land. The acres he eventually laid claim to became the ranch on which oil was found in the twenties. The first well became several dozen and they became Lucas Oil. But I still own the ranch."

"I've never been to Oklahoma." Mischievously, if with a straight face: "But I've seen the musical. Does the corn really grow as high as an elephant's eye?"

"I wouldn't know. We don't grow corn."

"Is it as beautiful as the Rocky Mountain states?"

"Well, the Wichita Mountains aren't as spectacular as the Rockies, but the prairie still has lots of wide open spaces, even now, and if you take Route One through the Ouachita National Forest it makes a beautiful drive in the fall, when the foliage is in full colour." Pause. "You liked the Rockies?"

"I have a thing about mountains. We have our own Scottish highlands but they're anthills compared to the mountain ranges of the United States."

"Charlie was born in the foothills of the Rockies."

"I know."

Luke contemplated her for moment then began: "Look, Fiona—" but a voice, mocking, resonant, over-rode whatever he had been going to say.

"My dear, dear Fiona. What a – dare I say pleasant? – surprise."

Luke saw Fiona's face whiten to the bone. For a moment there was sheer terror in her eyes then they blanked out, as if all life had been extinguished. She did not look up at the man who had stopped by their table and her voice was equally lifeless when she answered: "No, you may not."

"Still bearing grudges, I see."

"The very same ones you loaded me with."

She still hadn't looked up at him. Never would, Luke realised, but he did, at a staggeringly handsome man with the face of a Greek god and the body of an athlete. He had very blue eyes and hair the colour of a ripe horse-chestnut. Luke loathed him on sight.

"I had hoped you would be prepared to let bygones be bygones," he was saying reproachfully, sounding hurt.

"You are the only bygone I wish to be gone," Fiona said.

"Such a pity." The blue eyes turned to Luke. "So I suppose you're not going to introduce me to your – er – friend?"

"Why?" Fiona asked, in a voice suddenly sitting up and taking notice. "Still having trouble making any of your own?"

Luke saw an ugly look mar the vivid blue eyes but Fiona did not. She was still staring fixedly at the table-cloth.

"One thing, at least, hasn't changed," the Greek god said contemptuously. "You still use a serrated tongue. You may bear the grudges, Fiona, but I still bear the scars."

Turning on his heel, he stalked away.

Luke saw Fiona close her eyes and clutch at the table. He signalled the waiter. "Brandy – a double – and on the double – and hold dinner, OK?" Moving round the banquette, he put his arm around her. She was stiff as a board. "It's all right. He's gone."

She didn't answer. Her face was queerly white and there was perspiration on her brow and upper lip. The

brandy came and Luke put the glass to her lips. "Go on –
you need it."

She managed to take a few sips then shook her head.
When he put the glass down she turned to him blindly, as
though seeking refuge. Putting his arms around her, he
turned his body so as to shield her from curious eyes. As
always, she smelled of roses, but her softness was rigid
with sheer terror. He held her without speaking until the
rigidity melted into uncontrollable trembling.

"Say the word and I'll go belt that son of a bitch," he
offered.

"No!" It was a plea. "Rory is not man to tangle with.
He is both vicious and vindictive. He was also a boxing
blue at Cambridge."

"You obviously know him well. Old boyfriend?"

"Not old enough, and not a boyfriend. He was my
husband for six years." When the shock had faded from
Luke's eyes, she continued: "I managed to free myself of
him seven years ago. This is the first time I've seen him
since the divorce, which he has never accepted. He regarded – still regards – me as his legal and personal
possession. Something he owns, stamped with his brand:
'Property of Rory Ballater'." Letting out a shaky breath,
"I am so sorry," she apologised. "I've ruined your dinner
. . . It's just – he stirs up so many foul memories . . ."

"Why should you be apologising? None of this is your
fault."

Bleakly: "He has that effect on me. I was always
apologising to him for one thing or another."

"I'd still dearly love to go and try and ruin that
handsome profile."

"No! Please . . . I don't want to have anything to do with him in any way. He's the kind of man who never forgets. He—" She stopped abruptly and he saw her eyes go out of focus, heard her inhale sharply before staring blindly at something which was obviously blocking her view. Something shocking. Reaching for the brandy glass, she swallowed what was left in a gulp, set the glass down again and sat staring at it. He waited, sure more was to come.

"Rory is the ultimate in users," she said at last. "I didn't know this when I married him. I didn't know anything. I was young, naïve, desperately in love. I idolised him. When I discovered he was betraying me time and time again with God knows how many women – not in a careless, thoughtless way, but deliberately, callously, indifferently – I couldn't forgive him. This he could not understand. He thought his fatal attraction to women would always ensure his eventual triumph. He still refuses to accept that one of them – me – got away, and permanently, all because he took one of his women to Nice for the weekend when, by one of life's little ironies, my brother's ship was there on a courtesy visit. He saw Rory leaving the *Negresco* and when he went to the desk to enquire for me was told Mrs Ballater was upstairs in their suite. The woman who opened the door to him was someone my brother had never seen in his life. At last I had what I had longed for: uncontestable proof of his adultery, witnessed by enough people to be able to sue for divorce on those grounds and win. He never for one moment thought it would happen. It wasn't supposed to happen. Not to him. He had always charmed his way through life. Nobody had ever questioned his face value. We were all supposed to be so dazzled he could get away with murder. Even my mother – not easily taken in – had no idea of what lurked beneath the surface.

"I was only nineteen when we had a big, glittering, society wedding where I married him and he married the five hundred thousand pounds I inherited from my grandmother. His first betrayal was on our honeymoon. Once we were back from that he proceeded to spend every penny of my inheritance – on himself, of course. And once the money was gone he punished me for not having more to give him. By even more affairs. Oh, everyone thought we were the perfect couple – appearances matter terribly to him – but my marriage was a charnel-house. I tried to end it after three months. He punished me for that. And went on punishing me. He didn't want me any more but that didn't mean he would let me go. You see, the Ballater family motto is 'What I have I hold.' "

The convulsive trembling had subsided, but Luke could still sense deep, inner aftershocks.

She sat up straighter, smoothed her hair. "I'm sorry for all this but – I just wasn't prepared. I never thought to encounter him again if I could help it, and to do it here, of all places . . . It – he – took me unawares . . ."

"You weren't to know he'd be here."

"It's not the sort of place he would normally be found in; Rory has never done a day's work in his life." He felt as well as saw her shudder. "He has the power to stir up feelings best kept in cages. We are Celts, he and I, and our emotions are as fiery as our hair."

"Like how?"

She contemplated him. "Well, take my own family. Back in the seventeenth century there was a blood feud with another clan and the wife of the then Clan Sutherland chief was taken hostage. She was pregnant, almost to full term. As she was the wife of a clan chief she was treated with great ceremony, seated at the high table alongside the chief of the enemy clan. They laid before her a handsome dish, invited her to take off the cover and eat. When she did, on the plate lay her husband's head."

Luke's expression made her smile for the first time. "You see . . ."

"Indeed I do," he answered, thinking, A hell of a lot more than you realise. Like why you stepped back and away from Charlie. The likeness was not total, but the similarities were such as to make it clear that he and Rory Ballater were blood brothers.

"Could you manage some dinner now?"

A shudder. "No, thank you. Rory has quite spoiled my appetite. I would like to go upstairs, if you don't mind. Why don't you join your friends and eat with them . . ." She hesitated. "But would you do me one more favour first?"

"Name it."

"Would you see if Rory is registered here?"

"We don't have to stay, whether he is or not. We can leave right now . . ."

"I wouldn't dream of it. You came to the conference because you judged it to be necessary, and there is another day to go. We shall stay until its end. I only want to know about Rory for my peace of mind."

75

Which was tranquillised somewhat when it transpired that he was not a guest of the hotel. Even so, Luke accompanied her upstairs and insisted on checking her suite. "Lock your door if you want, and remember I'm right next door. Holler if you need me."

"I will." Gratefully she said: "Thank you so much for being there. I couldn't have coped with Rory on my own."

She locked her door behind him but for safety's sake placed a big chair in front of it. She was on the fifth floor, but she still checked the windows. With Rory Ballater it paid to take every precaution there was.

When at last she was safe in bed, a feeling of cold desolation swept over her. Meeting Rory had been frightening, but it had also been enlightening, in that it had showed her how right she had been to trust her instincts about Charlie. Her subconscious had recognised him as Rory under another name. Both men, she thought now, shared that honed edge of danger which obviously still held a powerful attraction for her. Why? Why did that particular type of man attract her? She no longer had the excuse of youth and inexperience. Yet she had still gone and done it again. Just as Rory had created needs and appetites which he had then proceeded to starve so that she was reduced to begging, becoming less and less of a woman and more of a dependent *thing*, so Charlie had followed the same game-plan. He had not taken her to bed that night after the nightclub, had deliberately not satisfied her as she had needed then to be satisfied, in spite of her doubts and reservations. Having hooked her he had played her a

76

little more, bringing her gradually to the stage where she would be in such a state as to allow him to do anything. And when she had told him to stay away, she now saw with the usual clarity of hindsight, she had secretly been hoping he would not take no for an answer. But he had been confident enough of her to do exactly that. Leaving her still on the hook, and gasping.

It seemed she was doomed to go on repeating her mistake. What is it with me and such men? she thought despairingly. I thought I had learned my lesson from Rory, so why did I let Charlie – his clone – get to me? What fatal weakness is there in me that finds bad lots so powerfully attractive? Why couldn't it have been Luke? He is – that nineteenth-century word for a very twentieth-century man – a gentleman: a gentle man. That casual cowboy/ruthless entrepreneur exterior conceals a kind, sensitive interior. There is no way he would knowingly hurt. Look how concerned for me he was tonight. Thank God I was with him rather than Charlie. He and Rory would have taken one look at each other, recognised a kindred spirit, and I'd have been done for.

It was no real satisfaction to know it but she was under no illusions now. Encountering Rory again had shone a very bright light on them, shown how threadbare they were. Thank you, Rory, she thought. I never thought to see the day, but you did me a favour by appearing tonight. Nevertheless she still lay wakeful until day was breaking.

She was quiet and withdrawn next day, though she did what was asked of her in her usual efficient way. There was no sign of Rory Ballater, and at four o'clock, when the conference wound up, Luke was impatient to be gone. He had got whatever it was he had come for; now it was time to go on to the next thing. Fiona was equally glad to be leaving, to put as much distance as possible between her and her ex-husband.

They were on their way by four thirty, Luke driving, and the big car purred effortlessly south. Still disturbed by her traumatic encounter and not having slept more than an hour or two the night before, she drifted off, and it was as they were coming down through the Northumberland moors that she began to talk in her sleep. She had been moving her head restlessly, making inarticulate murmurs, when suddenly, in her most crystalline voice, Luke heard her say clearly: "No, I will not do that!" Then, with less certainty: "No, I won't . . . I don't want to . . ." Then there was a sob and her voice begged: "Please, Rory, don't make me do that . . . please . . . No, don't . . ."

Luke's foot hit the brakes, and as he bent over her, huddled in her coat, she opened blurred eyes. In the dim light of the dashboard she saw only his shape looming over her and instinctively her arm went up to shield her face.

"Christ!" swore Luke instinctively, regretting more than ever that he hadn't smashed Rory Ballater's face in.

Fiona came fully awake then, and as her arm dropped, the face behind it went from paper-white to shamed crimson. "Sorry . . . bad dream," she explained rapidly, all but scuttling into herself, deeply mortified by her involuntary revelation.

"You were talking in your sleep."

"Was I? I haven't done that in a long time." She sat up. "What time is it?"

"Just after seven thirty. Newcastle ahead. I thought we'd stop there and have some dinner."

She wasn't hungry but knew he must be – lunch had been a sandwich and a beer – so she toyed with an omelette and drank a cup of coffee while he demolished a fillet steak and French fries. She refused a glass of the Fleurie he ordered to go with it, the reason becoming apparent when, as they walked back to the car, she said: "Why don't I drive for a while? I'm wide awake now."

"Sure," Luke agreed easily, divining at once her real reason: fear of falling asleep and exposing more of what he was coming to realise was a very well concealed cupboard chock-a-block with skeletons.

Fiona wasn't sure when he went to sleep. She only knew that as they bypassed Durham he was dead to the world. Once she hit the motorway she put her foot down and moved into the fast lane. The car fled south as if pursued by demons, and as she drove she wept silently, a weeping that did nothing to soften the hard core of her misery. She kept smearing away tears with the back of her hand, not wishing to stop and hunt for tissues in case she woke Luke. She wound down the window, hoping the wind would dry her face, until a glance at the speedometer showed her she was doing eighty.

Just beyond Doncaster they ran into rain, so she slowed even further: no sense in hurtling this big, powerful car across dangerously slippery surfaces. By Leicester they had left the rain behind so she increased speed again. That was when Luke woke up.

"Where are we?"

"That's Leicester over there."

"Want me to take over?"

"No. I'm all right if you are."

"Sure," he said again, closing his eyes once more.

The miles flew away under the wheels, but Fiona felt that she was the one who was being driven until, leaving the motorway at Hendon, she was conscious of her relief, as if the anonymity of the great city afforded sanctuary.

Stopping for a red light, she glanced at herself in the mirror. She was pale, quenched, tear-stained. Then she realised Luke was awake and watching her. "Not far now," she said, accelerating away as the lights changed.

"You OK? Not tired?"

"Not really, but I could go a cup or two of Henry's coffee."

"You and me both." He straightened his arms and legs in a luxurious stretch. "Come to that, as I recall there's nothing particular doing today, so why don't we take it off and take it easy at the same time. All that sitting and talking makes me restless. I feel the need for fresh air and a good horse."

"Whatever you say," she agreed, knowing what he was doing but too grateful to say anything but "Thank you." Adding simply: "For everything."

Six

B ack in harness again, Fiona began working with
Luke on the acquisition – done with such skill and
finesse as to make her aware she was attending a mas-
terclass – of the majority shareholding in a small independent oil producer named North Star. He did not
enlighten her as to why – he always played his cards not
so much close to his chest as from memory – so she
assumed it was because it had reserves which would
complement his own. Whatever his reason, the task
dominated her thoughts, which suited her just fine.

Nothing more had been said about her leaving. The
Aberdeen tremor and its subsequent aftershocks had
brought about a shift in the tectonic plates underlying
their relationship which left the reason in ruins. She had
come to admire Luke, to trust him, to respect him, faults
and all. Now she added gratitude to the tally. From the
beginning they had melded as friends, but that friendship
had mutated, after the run-in with Rory and her subsequent revelations, into something complicitous, a fact
of which Charlie was instantly aware.

For the first couple of weeks she was on tenterhooks in
case Rory tracked her down, but as the days passed and
there was no sign of him her fears subsided. Besides,

watching Luke at work pre-empted all else. When once he had acquired a large enough shareholding, North Star broke cover and ran for protection to one of the Seven Sisters, the huge multinational companies which dominated the oil business, which was when it was revealed that the small independent had found an apparently bottomless source of oil some 180 miles off the coast of Venezuela. Its share price soared accordingly, whereupon Luke unloaded his block for six times what he had paid for it, netting him a profit that took Fiona's breath away and which he promptly proceeded to use as capital in a whole raft of speculative ventures.

"How did you know?" Fiona asked him, curiosity burning bright. "About the discovery of the new field, I mean."

"I learned to track at an early age. By now I know what to look for."

Indeed you do, Fiona thought. You can spot signs nobody else so much as realises are there in the first place.

The blondes still came and went, though as time went on she noticed a gradual hiatus. When they were not entertaining or no friends had dropped in, Luke would not go out to the Clermont or Crockfords. He took to staying at home more, dining casually and contentedly in the kitchen with her and Henry, sometimes later on watching television, sometimes just talking, other times playing poker with Henry or Scrabble with him and Fiona. It was Charlie who went out now, and she was relieved. It was easier to deal with him on a strictly business basis.

And then, one morning at the beginning of November, Luke said: "It's Thanksgiving in a couple of weeks. I thought we'd have a party."

"Turkey and cranberry sauce and pumpkin pie?"

"All the trimmings. Henry knows the score. Will you organise everything else?"

"Just lead me to the guest list."

"I thought maybe, say, fifty people. A dozen or so to dinner and the rest afterwards."

Having a mother who was a famed Highland hostess, Fiona's preparations followed her precepts. Henry cooked two forty-pound American turkeys and a thirty-pound ham, ordered a sackful of massive Idaho potatoes for baking, and whipped up bowl after bowl of sour-cream-and-chives to go with them. He prepared dozens of corn-cobs for steaming, vast bowls of salad, towers of cornbread, umpteen pumpkin pies, trays of biscuits, a huge three-tier devil's food cake with inch-thick frosting, an equally big pound cake and dozens of brownies. He had all three ovens plus the microwaves going all day. Harrods' van delivered crates of champagne, and a college friend of Luke who was with the American Embassy arranged for the supply of cases of Mr & Mrs T. Bloody Mary Mix to go with the ocean of vodka, ditto cases of tequila and triple sec, plus a bag of air-freighted Florida limes to complete Henry's superlative margaritas, along with white rum for his daiquiris. The enormous living room was cleared for dancing, and Charlie supervised the setting-up of the multiple automatic-change CD player and its loudspeakers.

Eighteen people finally sat down at the extended

dining table at eight o'clock, and by ten the party guests
began to arrive. The majority were fellow-Americans,
but there was a sprinkling of Europeans and a goodly
leavening of gorgeous women, a fair selection of whom
Fiona recognised as members of Luke's harem.

She had organised it all down to the last olive, and
until things took off kept busy circulating, checking that
everyone had a glass and/or a plate, that the hired waiters
were doing their job, and that Henry was not getting
tennis elbow from his constant carving. The music was
snappy and the dancing under way. Floating here, there
and everywhere, she liaised with Henry at all times and
was smugly satisfied to see, after a while, that the party
had levelled off at around 35,000 feet.

From where he was standing on the sidelines, Charlie
reached out a lazy hand to capture her as she flitted by
him for the umpteenth time.

"Whoah . . ." he chided smoothly. "Take it easy.
Everything is already floating."

"That it is," chuckled the bald, round-faced, ever-
smiling man standing next to him. "Always is around
J. J. Lucas."

Fiona smiled at him, ignoring Charlie as she disen-
gaged herself politely but firmly from his hold. Fortunately, she needed do no more because just then a blonde
came up and took him away to dance.

"So you're Luke's English right hand," the plump
smiling man said.

"I help out."

"Some help, if what I hear is the truth of it. And some
party you've laid on."

"Thank you. I take it you're an old friend of Luke's?"

"And his daddy before him."

"Are you in oil too?"

"As a sideline. Mostly I'm a judge."

"Oh dear, but I suppose we *are* under American rule of law, considering the date. Have you made this American territory for the night? Isn't the Stars and Stripes above the buffet table large enough? I hung the biggest one I could find."

The plump, smiling man yelped with laughter. "Charlie said you were sassy."

"Of course, naturally you would know Charlie too."

"Almost as long as I've known Luke. Those two were joined at the hip even before Luke married Charlie's half-sister."

Accurately reading Fiona's expression: "He didn't tell you?" The judge nodded to himself. "Not surprising. It hit Luke so hard he probably still can't talk about it. His wife's death was a real tragedy . . . Such a waste of a truly beautiful girl." Enlightening Fiona once more: "She was killed in a hunting accident a few years back."

"Charlie's half-sister . . ." Fiona said, half to him, half to herself, staggered by the ramifications that particular fact revealed.

"Full-blooded Cheyenne, whereas Charlie is half white. Her tribal name was Star-that-Shines, but everybody called her Stella. Their mother married a second time when Charlie was four: Willard Whitesky, who ran the trade school on the Northern Cheyenne reservation. He adopted Charlie, who took his name, then Stella was born a year or so later. Willard was killed when a truck

85

filled with drunken rednecks drove his car off the road and into a ravine, so Charlie and his baby sister came with their mother to Oklahoma to keep house for Luke's daddy after his wife died. Lucy Whitesky raised all three children together, until they weren't children any more and Luke and Stella fell in love."

The judge's pause filled in a whole lot more of the blanks in Fiona's crossword. "I guess you could say things were pretty bad between Luke and Charlie after Stella was killed."

As light illuminated a situation about which she had known only half-truths, Fiona stared in shock at the whole truth now revealed. Charlie blamed – was still blaming – Luke for the death of his half-sister.

"It was a tragic accident," the judge was saying; "everybody knew that, and the inquiry confirmed it, but Charlie set great store by his sister . . . Still, like they say, time heals all things. Luke is the proof of that. It makes me real glad to see they've patched things up."

Not with Charlie using his knife on the stitches, Fiona thought.

"Losing Stella the way he did purely took the heart out of Luke. He had us all worried for a while, but I can see things are back to normal." The smile reappeared. "Thanks in no small part to you, so Henry tells me."

"Henry tends to exaggerate," Fiona demurred, wondering, What did I do? "If ever a man knew what he was doing at all times it is John J. Lucas – and as you know him so well, what does the second J stand for? I can't get him to tell me."

The judge chuckled. "Not surprising. He hates the

name. He's named for his great-great-grandfather, the one who founded the Double J Ranch. John Jeremiah."

Fiona winced. "No wonder he prefers to be called Luke." Then she flashed him a smile, grateful to him for a lot of vital information. "Now, if you'll excuse me, I must circulate, see that everyone is taken care of."

"You go on about your business," the judge said indulgently. "We'll talk again later, I hope. You live up to your reputation."

"I wasn't aware I had one," flashed Fiona, in no doubt as to which of the dynamic duo had spun the tale. It wasn't Luke's style.

She headed for the kitchen, where it would be less noisy, and there found Henry preparing to set up the second turkey, the first one having been carved to a skeleton.

"How you doin'?" he greeted her.

"Just fine. The party has really taken off."

"The amount of liquor they're puttin' away, I won't be surprised when they do the same." He eyed her narrowly. "You OK?"

"Yes, fine. I just thought I'd catch my breath a moment."

"Set yourself down. Take five – or ten, come to that."

Like the magician he was, he quickly placed in front of her a tall, well-iced gin and tonic.

"Henry, you unfailingly do the right thing," she told him gratefully.

"Why not? You do right by us. I ain't seen Luke so chipper in a coon's age."

Which was exactly what the judge had said, but there

was no way she could take credit. He had just made a not-so-small fortune on the North Star deal so it was no wonder he was chipper.

"He has a lot of irons in his particular fire right now," she agreed, "all heating up very satisfactorily. I don't know how he keeps track of them all."

"I do," Henry said. "He graduated from Princeton *summa cum laude.*"

Another surprise. Tonight was turning out to be full of them. Especially Star-that-Shines. What a lovely name. As lovely as its bearer, according to the judge. And everything to Luke. The implication was that he had been devastated. Was that the reason for the transient blondes? Having lost the one woman who meant everything, he couldn't bring himself to commit a second time in case he lost her too?

While Charlie blamed him.

Yes. Stella was the keystone of this particular triangle.

Why, then, this feeling of loss and hurt? Probably because, in spite of her soul-baring in Aberdeen, Luke had not said understandingly: "I know how you feel, because I too know what it is like to lose someone and something on which you have staked your all."

Only mine had died long before I managed to throw it out, Fiona thought. Luke's had obviously still been in full flower when the Grim Reaper's scythe sliced it off. I'm willing to lay any odds that Stella's hair was every bit as raven black as her brother's. That's why they're always blondes . . .

He can't bring himself to talk about her, she thought. Not even to me . . . not even after Aberdeen . . . I

88

thought he trusted me as I trust him, but Stella is obviously a memory too precious to be shared with anyone. Unconsciously she sighed.

Henry eyed her thoughtfully. He knew that brooding expression by now. Somethin' was gettin' to her and he'd bet any odds it was Charlie, sharpening his knife so as to make another notch on a belt that had to be wearin' thin by now, it had been cut so often.

Aware of his scrutiny, Fiona emptied her glass before saying with determined brightness: "Right, recess over. I must go back and do some more hostessing. Thank you for the drink, Henry. It was just the restorative I needed."

As she went back into the living room she saw the dancing was in full swing. Luke was cheek to cheek with a blonde who had hair the colour of sunshine and a tan that spoke of sunbeds, well displayed by a tight, white dress that was cut down to the cleft of her buttocks. Fiona swung sharply away, only to collide with Charlie, who had materialised behind her.

"Where have you been hiding?" he complained. "The music is going to waste." Before she could resist he had her in his arms and on the dance floor, totally unprepared. Avoidance had been the better part of valour since Aberdeen. Fitting her tight against him, he murmured: "Oh, how I've missed this . . ."

"You should have told me," she countered sarcastically, refusing to allow her treacherous body to go into meltdown.

"I did."

"Only what suited you."

89

"It would have suited me to be able to visit with you and your mother, but I never got the chance."

"Jealous?"

"Envious."

They made a spectacular couple. People watching commented on it. Charlie's copper handsomeness set off Fiona's cameo fragility, her wine-dark hair glowing above a dress that was a drift of smoke-blue organza. They moved together in perfect unison, through one dance and straight into another.

"Charlie getting ready to *count coup*?" the judge asked Luke from where they stood on the sidelines.

"Fiona knows too much about Native Americans to allow that," Luke answered shortly.

"Looks like Charlie's hoping to teach her a lot more. What's the matter? Lost your touch? That's one good-looking woman. Smart too."

Luke didn't answer. He was watching Charlie slowly but deliberately dancing Fiona down to the far end of the room until they were right outside the jib-door that led to her office. In a trice he had opened it, whisked her through and shut it behind them.

The judge turned as if to say, "Didn't I tell you?", but the expression on Luke's face stilled his tongue.

Fiona had been concentrating so hard on holding Charlie at bay emotionally that she was unaware of his physical strategy until she found herself being held tightly and kissed with naked passion in a dark room, the object of a sudden, almost violent, assault. This was not Charlie deliberately setting out to arouse, this was Charlie already aroused, to a state which evoked in her not an equal passion but rather shock and alarm. Struggling to free herself: "Charlie! Please . . . you're hurting me . . . Charlie, for God's sake!" She heard her pleas echoing down the years to another time, another man but the same situation. 'No, please, Rory, don't . . . you're hurting me . . .' Memory gave her the added strength to wrench herself free. "I meant what I told you before," she told him shakily. "You're bad medicine for me."

"What the hell do you think you're doing to me?"

"I'm no match for you and you know it! I tried to go the distance once before with someone too like you for comfort, and got beaten to a pulp."

"This is a mistake?" He advanced, but she retreated behind her desk. "Don't play with me, Fiona," he warned, and she saw just how dangerous he could be.

"You're the one who's playing."

"What – or who – gives you that idea?"

"It's no longer an idea. It's a cast-iron certainty."

"Is this an example of your famous Celtic precognition?"

"No. Just good old-fashioned common sense. I've been there, Charlie. My calluses come from hard use."

"You sound like he was a combination of Casanova and Jack the Ripper."

"He was." She paused before continuing: "You remind me of him so much."

He regarded her unreadably. Finally: "Is that why I can't get you to trust me?" Before she could answer he went on persuasively: "You're throwing us away, Fiona. We could have been good together."

"At what?"

"You name it, we could have had it."

"No hearts and flowers, please. 'Hail to the Chief' is more in your line."

"What do I have to do to win you, Fiona?"

"Play an honest game."

His smile made her flinch. "We always lost when we did that." She forced herself to stand still under his probing gaze, could almost hear the ball clicking as he calculated his bet for the next spin of the wheel.

"All right," he agreed finally. "We'll abandon this game. Just remember that the series isn't even half over."

As the door closed behind him Fiona fell shakily into her chair. Her legs had liquefied and she was all of a flutter inside, for while her mind knew she had done the right thing he had, as always, left her body clamouring for him. She was still sitting there in total darkness when the door opened again, letting in a stream of light which lit her like a spot. Against it, Luke's body was a stony silhouette.

"Some people are leaving," he said in voice that applied an ice-cold compress to her overheated emotions. Skin-crawlingly conscious of his eyes, she rose from her chair to sweep past him without a word.

For the rest of the evening she avoided Charlie. She danced and talked and laughed and was conscious of him down to every toe and fingernail. He watched her steadily and it unnerved her. Catching sight of herself in a mirror, she saw she was hectically flushed, eyes enormous with a febrile glitter. As she looked, she saw Charlie in the background. Meeting her eyes, he held them. And smiled.

Seven

I t was almost 3 a.m. by the time the last guests had gone tipsily on their way, leaving behind the skeletons of the two turkeys and the shining bone of the ham, along with the debris of dirty plates, glasses and coffee cups, overflowing ashtrays, a fug of smoke and various kinds of perfume. Fiona went round flinging wide all the windows, and it was as she was leaning out of one on the upper level, inhaling the fresh pre-dawn air, that she heard, coming from below her, Luke's molten-with-rage voice.

"Just what the hell kind of a game are you playing here, Charlie?"

There was a ten-second silence, as though Charlie had turned to survey Luke at leisure before answering, at his most insolent: "I don't question how much you lose at poker. What I do in my own time is none of your business, and *business* partners is all we are, remember?"

"When you're using Fiona Sutherland as a pawn then it *is* my business, because she works for me. Don't mess this – and her – up, Charlie."

"Or you'll do what?" The insolence cracked like a whip. Then his voice changed, seeming to curl at the edges. "Fiona is old enough to know what she's doing . . . and she does it very well, believe me . . ."

Up on the balcony, Fiona cringed.

"You bastard!" Luke's voice sounded as though it came from between clenched teeth. "I know how you operate. God knows I've seen it often enough. You get them so close to the edge they have only one way to go – and that's over it!"

"Ah, but Fiona is a very well-balanced female."

"Not right now. She's as vulnerable as hell and I won't stand for you making things worse."

"What do you mean?" Charlie picked up on the reference at once.

"None of *your* business. I'm warning you, Charlie. Lay off this one!"

"Why not Fiona?" Charlie sounded as if he was choosing a tie, but Fiona knew that it was when he sounded most indolent that he was at his most alert. "She's the greatest challenge I've met in a long time."

"And you always have to meet and beat them, don't you?"

"I don't tell you how to handle your blondes."

"I don't give them a snow job! They know what I want and it never goes any further."

"And we both know why, don't we?"

In the sudden, crackling silence Fiona prayed fervently: Belt him, Luke. Please, do to Charlie what you wanted to do to Rory. Smash his smug face in!

But she heard instead the sound of rapid footsteps along the parquet floor in the direction of the door, which slammed shut violently. That was Luke. Charlie never slammed doors.

Fiona forced herself to breath-holding rigidity,

smothering any sound she might make in the heavy folds of the bronze velvet curtains. She heard the clink of ice in a glass, the gurgle of liquid as it was poured, then a soft footfall and the door opening and closing again as Charlie left. Only then, and carefully, inch by stealthy inch, did she peer over the balustrade. The room was empty. In a flash she was off and running.

With her door safely shut – and locked, since there were combustible emotions abroad tonight – she paced back and forth in a humiliated rage. This was the last straw! If they wanted proof, all they had to do was check her broken back. Enough was enough! This was most definitely no longer any place for her. Acting on her decision, she went to the closet where her cases were stored and began to pack.

Oh boy, had she ever been right about Charlie Whitesky! He was up to no good, all right. Which brought her up short against the blank screen of just what he *was* up to. Only to find, as she stared at it, that there was a picture forming. One that showed her something she did not like because she did not wholly understand it. Luke was afraid of Charlie.

She sank down on her bed in disbelief. She would have sworn – on any stack of Bibles – that J. J. Lucas was not the kind of man you could scare. He thrived on danger. Look at the financial risks he took on a daily basis.

Yes, *financial* risks, her inner voice reminded her. This thing with Charlie has nothing whatever to do with business. This is personal. Deeply personal. It has to do with Star-that-Shines – Luke's wife and Charlie's half-sister. Her death and the manner of it is what lies between those two, which means that if Charlie's feelings are so deep and dark that he feels a need to wreak revenge then it has to have been a disastrous, unforgettable – probably unnecessary – death.

Fiona felt a chill.

The judge had said it was a hunting accident, but they came in a whole range of styles and shapes. Had it been a careless one? A stupid one? An unthinking one? *An avoidable one?* Fiona had been brought up with guns; as a girl she had spent too many long hours in a butt or crouched on a skyline not to be aware of just how dangerous shotguns could be. But if it was an accident, as the judge maintained, why was Charlie holding Luke responsible? For not taking enough care, perhaps? For taking his wife – *Charlie's sister* – into a dangerous situation? Whatever the reason, it was enough for Charlie to be adding compound interest to what Fiona now understood, with aching pity, to be Luke's already crippling debt of guilt.

She chewed on a nail. There was far more here than even she had bargained for, but as she tried to take it in, what stood square in her path, arms folded like some threatening bouncer, was the rightness of her conclusions about Charlie. The only reason for his pursuit of her was to get at Luke. Which again brought her up short, because that presupposed an interest on Luke's part.

Her mother's daughter, Fiona had inherited many of the facets of her typical Scots character: her astute, even fey, reading of people; her quick-wittedness; her down-to-earth practicality allied to a well-furnished imagination; and her ability to intuit the diamonds in a pile of pebbles. Take it back to the beginning, she told herself now, and look for clues.

Charlie's "campaign" had begun the night they found Luke drunk; therefore that fact had been the signal to attack. But *why* had Luke been drunk? What was he trying to escape from? An unhappy anniversary? Yet next day he'd acted as though it had never happened. So it wasn't that. But had that lapse been the reason for the diamond rose? And had it been a peace offering or a bribe?

Don't be ridiculous, she slated herself in the next breath. Luke has no need to bribe any woman to spend time with him. But he had never risen to Charlie's bait, never asked her out. Yet in Scotland he had displayed evident satisfaction at her cutting Charlie off at the knees. Which brought her full circle to the sixty-four-thousand-dollar question. If Charlie was so bent on revenge, why did Luke keep him around? What was it he had said? "You get them so close to the edge the only place to go is over it." He had also said, "Not this one." Which meant Charlie had done it before. How many times? And why?

She rubbed her forehead as if attempting to unblock an information flow, but the trouble was that, even now, there was still so much she did not know.

So deep was she in her thoughts that the knock on her door made her jump convulsively.

"Fiona? You all right?"

Marvelling at the even tenor of her voice: "Yes. Thank you, Luke. Sorry I didn't say good-night. It was a fine party."

There was a short silence, then: "Yeah . . . You did your usual great job. Thanks. Good-night."

She checked his voice for traces of sarcasm and/or contempt but found none. Only sincerity.

Oh, hell, she thought frustratedly. How could she walk out without so much as an explanation? She owed him that, at least. Luke was a kind man. Charlie hadn't come to see if she was all right. It was Luke who was concerned for her.

She held that thought. *Luke?* Was it possible? No, never! From the start he had flirted, teased, but nothing . . . *meant.* And though he might lack Charlie's stunning good looks and cat-like grace of movement, he was still a very attractive man. Her mother had thought so. But then, her mother hadn't seen Charlie . . . No woman would ever see Luke when Charlie was around. Except when they were paid to, of course . . .

Something hovered in the background of her mind but she couldn't get a grip on it to bring it forward for examination. It's all far too complicated, she thought restlessly. Trouble was, those complications had wound her to a pitch where she knew she wouldn't be able to sleep for thinking about them. What she needed was something to render her unconscious. Which was when she remembered the laden table downstairs. Enough liquor to put an army to sleep. A double slug of Jack Daniels and she'd be out like a light. But that would be giving in, acknowledging her own lack of control. No, she thought. Ignore the "Candy is dandy but liquor is quicker" bit. Have a long soak in a hot bath filled with Jo Malone's luxurious bubbles. That always works.

But tonight it didn't. Nor did a hundred soothing strokes with the hairbrush. She was wide awake and as tight as an overwound spring. So be it, she thought, Jack Daniels will just have to loosen it.

Wrapping herself in a silk kimono, she opened her door quietly. All was dark. Everyone had gone to bed. In her bare feet she padded noiselessly down the stairs and into the living room, lit only by the streetlamps but well enough to show her the long table, crowded with bottles and glasses. She went straight to the Jack Daniels, poured herself a generous two ounces and tossed it straight back. It hit her like a bolt of lightning. Coughing and spluttering, she wiped her eyes so that she could see enough to pour herself a refill, which she would take with her. If she drank it here she might not make it back up the stairs. Holding the brimming glass carefully, she turned to retrace her steps – only to find Luke standing at the end of the table, regarding her with a gaze that stopped her in her tracks. He looked as he had the night she found him sprawled in the big chair – jacket off, tie loosened – but this time he wasn't drunk. Nevertheless, her heart sank when he raised his own glass in an ironic salute. "Welcome to the club."

It spurred her into retorting: "I couldn't sleep. I thought perhaps a drink . . ."

"*A* drink? That's your second belt you're carrying."

Haughtily: "So take it out of my salary!"

She made to stalk past him but he reached out a hand to grasp her arm and turn her to him. As she resisted, the bourbon slopped over the brim of her glass to splash over her hand.

"Oops! Sorry. I know how important every last drop is. Here, let me get you a refill." Still keeping his firm grip on her arm, he drew her back to the bottle of Jack Daniels, where he set down his own glass before filling an eight-ounce tumbler to the brim. "There," he said, taking the jigger from her and replacing it with the tumbler. "That ought to do it. If you're that desperate it takes more than you think."

His voice, knowingly taunting, flicked her where it hurt: her pride.

"I am not *that* desperate."

"Liar," he said without heat.

"It's far too much," she insisted angrily.

"It's never enough."

"Well, you ought to know!"

She saw his face darken. "Jesus, your ex was right! You do have a serrated tongue!"

"If you will kindly let go of my arm I shall go back to my room and you need suffer it no longer."

"Oh, I suffer from a lot of things. What do you suffer from – apart from a case of the hots?"

Fiona gasped in shock, before pulling herself together to rally gamely: "Insomnia!"

He laughed at her. "Liar. Charlie is what you are suffering from – or should I say lack of Charlie."

Fiona felt the anger inside her turn sour with dismay. He had her dead to rights, but "None of your business," she returned mechanically.

"With Charlie shoving it down my throat?"

The clear eyes were a-glitter with a look that made her skin crawl with humiliation, spurring her to spit: "Then choke on it!" before jerking her arm free so violently that the contents of the tumbler went flying, mostly over her, drenching her throat and running in rivulets into the V-neck of her kimono, soaking her breasts.

"Now look what you've done!"

Her wrathful voice faded as she saw his eyes following the liquid running down her flesh to soak into the silk of her kimono, causing it to cling damply, outlining the firm thrust of her breasts, chilling her nipples into stiffness, for underneath her robe she wore only a thin silk nightdress. She saw his breath catch in his chest and the clarity of his eyes darken to smoke, the look in them turning her away from him in a sudden panic to escape. But he still had hold of her arm. In a dream-like fashion he reached out to pluck the all-but-empty glass from her palsied hand and set it down on the table, his attention so concentrated on her that he dropped it short. It fell to the carpet to roll away, unseen, unheard. Their attention had become welded to each other in an awareness that hummed like a high-voltage cable. Fiona could not have moved if she'd tried. In the same dream-like manner he put down his own glass before reaching out to grasp her other arm, drawing her to him. Slowly, oh so slowly, he brought her right up against him before bending his blond head to lick her damp flesh, murmuring in a thick, languid voice: "What a waste of good bourbon . . ."

Fiona arched convulsively as his mouth and tongue acted like a match on the alcohol in her bloodstream, causing it to explode into a blaze. Frantically she tried to lean backwards, but there was no escaping the deadly progress of that heat-seeking mouth and tantalising tongue, or the trail of liquid fire they left across her damp flesh, making her buck and gasp. One of his hands left her arm to pull at the loosely tied belt of her kimono, which fell open, allowing him to push it away from her shoulders so that it exposed her nightdress: a high-waisted fall of rose-red silk with a bodice – damply clinging now – of blond filigree lace, through which her chilled nipples jutted stiffly. He covered one of them with his mouth. Fiona's body erupted.

Time had thickened, congealed into a state of turgid slow motion. The only thing that raced was their hearts as they careered at breakneck speed down the slippery slope of sexual excitement.

"You're all wet," he murmured dreamily, his mouth hot and insidious, will-weakening and senses-provoking. Too much was happening too fast, Fiona thought blur-redly. This was *Luke!* This was not how it was meant to be, but all she could think of, all she could *feel*, was the progress of that insistent, heart-stopping mouth as it travelled with tantalising slowness upwards from her breasts towards her throat, and from there to her own mouth. Where it stopped. Raising his head he looked into her eyes. His were hot, fierce, the ice having melted to liquid mercury, and they locked on to hers like a heat-seeking missile. Then, still in that dream-like, slow-motion way, he covered her mouth with his own.

When she felt his tongue Fiona stiffened, pushing against him with the flat of her hands. It was like trying to overturn a tank. His mouth devoured hers and she could feel herself going under as the kiss deepened, triggering a response which burst its banks. Its effect on him was to loosen his grip on her upper arms so as to bring her more fully into his own. She could hear someone moaning, then she realised with shock that it was her, drowning in sensation and going down for the third time. The last thing she remembered, as the bourbon and Luke combined to kick her feet out from under her, were her own arms going up to lock behind his neck as she not only accepted his kiss but returned it passionately, grinding her hips against the length and thickness of his steely hardness. The long-smouldering fuse of frustration Charlie had ignited went off in a searingly hot flare of eroticism which sent her up, up and away – right over the edge.

Eight

F iona lay on her back, staring up at the ceiling. Beside her, Luke was sprawled on his stomach, his face buried in her shoulder, one arm flung across her, deeply asleep.

She was in a state of ravaged despair. What *had* she been thinking of? *Thinking!* her inner self flung back at her. You weren't capable of thinking once you'd been clobbered by feelings set free after years in solitary! *Idiot! Fool!* He was drunk and you were handy. In your oh-so-scrupulous avoidance of being used by Charlie you've ended up being used by Luke. How's that for a laugh? He didn't even know who you were!

Her throat clogged and her eyes welled as she recalled his voice, hoarse with love and longing, rising to an exultant shout as he climaxed: "*Stella, oh my love, Stella . . .*"

Filled with self-castigating despair, she gazed stonily up at the shadows of the ceiling, seeing only the ruins she had created. Which is what happens when – as Luke had sussed from the start – you get the hots for one man and end up in bed with another. Serves you damned well right. *Stella*, he had called her. *Stella!*

You and your damned need of a drink, she accused

herself, but even as she did so she felt her stomach drop and her heart stumble at the memory of what that drink had led to. She would have expected Charlie to be so expert, so skilled, but whereas his policy was to create appetites which he then assiduously starved, Luke had satisfied completely.

Fiona had learned about sex from a man who knew it all, a man who would stop at nothing in the pursuit of the ultimate in orgasms, especially his attendance – accompanied by his unwilling wife – at "swinging" parties, where sex was the order of the day and every kind of depravity practised; orgies that left her feeling dehumanised. And always, with Rory, no matter how passionate the sex, there had been that saw-toothed edge of cruelty lying in wait behind even his most seemingly tender words and actions. Not so Luke. There had been no hint of cruelty there, only passion – and such passion . . . Just the thought of what he'd brought her to, made her *feel*, had her stomach taking another turn for the worse. Without so much as a hint of the sexuality and sensuality which surrounded Charlie like a force field, Luke had opened up to revealed a motherlode of both. The sex truly had been incredible. For both of them, she reminded herself, for whatever he had given her – and he was the most generous of lovers – she had made sure he received in turn. The result had been heart-stoppingly rapturous, the more so for being unexpected.

So what? You were starved! she threw at herself, and frustrated as hell. He only had to lay a finger on you and you went off like a Catherine wheel.

Only to be called Stella.

She felt as if she'd been mugged. Robbed of identity, importance, self. And she had undergone enough of that with Rory. Luke's . . . defection had only served to further carve up a self-esteem that had been under the knife far too often. She had expected that, drunk or not, he would have known who she was.

Self-pitying tears oozed from her eyes. She had been classified in the same league as the blondes: just another body. Which is what you get for trying to pull a fast one. Oh yes, you did! Don't deny it. You knew – deep down where it matters you *knew* that, after that run-in with Charlie, Luke was likely to be up and about. Your need of a drink was in reality your need of sex. What you really wanted was to get rid of the frustration Charlie had engendered, only Luke used you because he can't get rid of his. Now there's a laugh for you!

Except the last thing she wanted to do was laugh. What she wanted and what she had received had not been so much as introduced to each other. She had not been able to see the stud for the tease.

Ha ha! she thought sourly. Rationalise it all you like. Parade your excuses. Give them all twenty-eight days' detention; black is still black and that is the colour of your anything-but-true love's hair.

The ache inside her was a hot, hard stone, forcing out tears every bit as hot, which rolled down her cheeks to drip from her chin on to Luke's own closed eyes, waking him. He blinked, and though every vestige of alcohol had been burned away, for one brief moment he wasn't sure where he was. Until he inhaled the familiar fragrance of roses. At once, memory kicked in, flooding his mind with a sequence of events that had begun with spilled whisky and gone on to damply clinging rose-red silk and –

"Fiona," he murmured gladly, moving closer to the warmth and fragrance. What they had done together, become together, had been real, not just another fantasy.

"No!" The violence of her voice matched the way she flung his arm away, but before she could leap out of bed he had his arm back across her, pinning her down.

"Wait a minute . . . What's brought this on? Why the injured party act?"

"How would you know where I hurt?"

"I hurt you?" Disbelief resonated.

"Not where it shows."

He frowned, as if trying to remember, before asking: "What did I do, for God's sake? You weren't complaining a while back – far from it . . ."

"How would you know *what* I was doing when you didn't even know *who* I was?"

He didn't move but suddenly he was no longer with her. She could tell by the difference in the weight of his arm, the tension which crackled about him like lightning. Then he removed himself from her physically, rolling away to the far side of his king-size bed. "Why should that bother you?" he demanded with brutal frankness. "Do you think I didn't know you were pretending I was Charlie? We were both fielding substitutes."

Her hand cracked across his face like the snap of a whip, the full weight of her arm behind it. His eyes blurred and his ears rang.

"You bastard!" Fiona's wet eyes were blazing like neon signs. "That's not true and you know it! All right, so it may have started out that way but you damned well know I didn't carry it through. I knew who *you* were all the time!"

She flounced out of the bed, all humiliated rage and hurt, and though his own anger had risen like a soufflé, he still noticed how warm and rosy and bed-tumbled she was, her wine-dark, silken hair spilling about her creamy shoulders, her pink-fondant-tipped breasts quivering in her rage as she fumbled with her nightdress, her surprisingly full and rounded body flushed with the heat of her emotions. Which was when it all swept over him: the feel of that body under his, the passionate giving of it, the unrestrained and unstinting response, most of all her voice saying his name – Luke – over and over again. Oh, Christ! he thought despairingly, putting his head into his hands. It seemed that what he'd thought of as his release had been nothing more than removal to another cell. Which was when he knew there was no way he could stand to be stuck in this new cell for the rest of his life. He was already stir-crazy. He took a deep breath and the chance of his life before saying flatly, "Stella was my wife. I killed her."

He saw her jerk and then stiffen. For a full ten seconds she didn't move. When she did turn to face him he saw that her tears had frozen on her shocked face. In turn, Fiona looked at a man recalling horrors he was still struggling to accept: face bloodless, eyes stark.

"It was an accident. We were out hunting a mountain lion that had been killing cattle. She must have disturbed a rattler because it struck at her – we found the venom in her boot, just by her ankle – and she must have panicked because she stood up and moved right into my sights just as I was squeezing the trigger . . . There was nothing I could do, no way I could stop it . . ."

In a voice constrained by his eternal internal struggle to accept the unacceptable: "You wanted to know what lies between me and Charlie. Stella's death does. He's never forgiven me for it and never will. He has been punishing me ever since, though God knows he has no need to. I've had to live with what I did every day of my life since."

As if his words had pressed a spring, Fiona dropped her nightdress and flung herself back on to the bed, scrambling across to pull him to her, wrapping her arms around him as though to warm him with the heat of her body. He was stiff and cold, but his arms went around her as though holding on to life itself.

"I'm sorry if I hurt you by thinking you were her . . . It was just – it's been a long time since it was like it used to be with her. This was the very first time, in fact, since her death. That's probably why I—"

Fiona placed her hand over his mouth, cutting off his words so as to spill out her own. "Oh God, I'm sorry, so very sorry. I had no idea . . ."

"Why should you? It's not something I go around telling people. You're the first person I have told, apart from the therapist I went to afterwards." There was a silence, but its quality told Fiona he wasn't finished. So she waited, holding him close, willing her warmth into him, until be began to tell her how he, Stella and Charlie had made the trip to Colorado to stay with friends who owned a ranch near the Rocky Mountain National Park.

For some time the friends had been steadily losing cattle to an obviously old and experienced mountain lion, so they had decided to form a hunting party to go out looking for it. Both Charlie and Luke were experienced trackers, added to which they had the dogs. Between them they had tracked the lion to a gully, into which it had disappeared, among rocks that were the same colour as it was. They had split up, Charlie, Stella and another man making up one party, Luke and two other men the second. The gully was a dead-end, so Luke and his companions had remained by its entrance so as to be ready if and when Charlie's group managed to drive the mountain lion down towards them.

"Stella had hunted with us since we were teenagers; she was a good shot and knew better than to expose herself to danger, so when they flushed the cougar and I saw it coming down the draw towards me I was the first one to have it in my sights – I knew I couldn't miss and I was actually squeezing the trigger when suddenly Stella appeared right between me and the lion. I could see her mouth was open as if she was either screaming or about to scream then suddenly I'd taken the shot and there was no face . . ."

Oh dear God, thought Fiona, sickened at the horror of it, knowing he was reliving it all again, seeing his wife's lovely face become a red mulch of blood and bone.

"I was . . . out of things for a while, but afterwards, when I got back on my feet and looked to do what they said I should do – make a fresh start – Charlie wouldn't let me. You know about Native Americans and their beliefs, how often there is a connection between mourning and war. That's what Charlie's been doing ever since: making war on me. Afterwards, and it was a long time afterwards, when I felt – was able to feel again, and began to make moves towards getting back to some kind of normal life, he wouldn't let me. Any woman I showed even the slightest interest in, he'd move in and take her away from me. You know how he can be, how he can focus on you in such a way that you can't see anything for his dazzle. He used it to – to geld me. The worst thing you can do to a man is destroy his belief in himself, so that it gets to the point where he daren't put himself on the line for fear of yet another rejection. Then he sticks to paying for what he needs: nothing more than physical release and the emptiness that comes afterwards." Hence the blondes. Fiona was so horrified by the cruelty in the picture he had drawn that she was speechless. She had indeed not known the half of it. What she did know, though, and from her own bitter experience, was how it felt to have your self-confidence deliberately sabotaged, all the separate compartments of self tipped upside-down, their contents strewn carelessly all over the place before being trodden on.

"And then I met you," Luke was saying, "and I think that subliminally I must have recognised you as somebody who had undergone their own suffering. You were outwardly so got-together, but I sensed there was so much more to you than capability and unflappable expertise. I thought I'd kept it under wraps, but Charlie knows my every reaction by now so naturally he moved in. Only you backed away from him, something that had never happened before, which made me hope that maybe you knew what he was doing. That's why I came to Scotland for you . . . I thought maybe we could straighten things out; but meeting Ballater in Aberdeen showed me only too clearly why Charlie had struck out."

He looked at her then, and she saw that some of the strain had eased. "We were both walking wounded," he said simply. "That was what I recognised in you."

"I had no idea," Fiona admitted guiltily. So much for her vaunted perception.

"How could you, with Charlie blocking your view at every turn?"

Right again, thought Fiona.

Encouraged by her rueful smile of acknowledgement, Luke possessed himself of her hands. "I want – I need – you to know how much this – tonight – has meant to me. I know it started because of Charlie but it was *me* you let love you, and *me* you loved back. Tonight you have helped me find myself again, not just a body but . . . the man I am, the one I thought Charlie had done for. Do you understand what I'm saying? This is the first time since Stella that making love to a woman has had an emotional content. That's why I called you by her name: because it was like it was with her – so much more than just sex – except that you are you and could never be anyone else. I've fantasised about you for a long time now."

Fiona was dumbfounded. How well he had hidden it! But then, with Charlie on the warpath . . . "I'm sorry I turned on you," she apologised. "I didn't understand, added to which I had my own lack of self-confidence."

"Like I said, walking wounded, the both of us." He

kissed her hands. "I knew you'd be good for me and I hated Charlie for pre-empting the approach I was nerving myself to make."

"Was that why you were drunk that night?"

"Partly; mostly because I'd just failed with a woman. Charlie had made me as impotent as he wanted me to be."

Now Fiona understood. The J. J. Lucas who was Superman when it came to his work was not the J. J. Lucas who was a rag-bag of doubts and insecurities when it came to his standing as a man. Fiona had learned about the male ego from Rory and knew only too well what a fragile bloom it was. Luke's had been deliberately deprived of the life-giving success men needed where women were concerned. It had been in such short supply for so long he was starving.

"I know you don't have much faith in men after your lousy marriage," Luke was saying, "but I would never hurt you. You mean too much to me. You're spunky, feisty as hell and utterly loyal. You're clever and quick and funny and very, very beautiful. The first time I set eyes on you I thought, Wow! And when I got to know you, the more I knew the more I wanted us to get together. When you dropped Charlie I had the glimmerings of hope, so I decided I'd fly to Aberdeen and try my luck, only you got mad with me and then Ballater ruined it all . . . But it was me you turned to for support, so I thought, Well, maybe, with time and patience . . . I wanted – still want – so much to be the only one with you just as I want you to be the only one with me."

Fiona's silence had him drawing back to say flatly:

"You think I'm crowding you." He dropped her hands, moved away from her. "Yeah, well, one roll in the hay doesn't make a stack."

Fiona took a firm hold on his chin, turning his face towards hers. "It was more than that for me too. Why else do you think I was so hurt when you called me Stella?"

For long moments they looked at each other, and then Luke took her into his arms and kissed her willing mouth. When they made love again it was an unforgettable feast of feeling and emotion which left them exhausted and capable of no more than lying entwined in replete silence.

After a while Fiona asked: "There is one other thing you could tell me, if you will. Why is Charlie doing this to you? Why is revenge so important to him?"

Luke's reply was unhesitating. "Because he was – is – as much in love with Stella as I was, maybe even more."

So that was it.

Jealousy.

Of course, thought Fiona. It was so simple.

Once you knew.

"Trouble was, to Stella, Charlie was only ever her brother. She hero-worshipped him, but it was me she loved. Once she became my wife he turned from my closest friend into my deadliest enemy, but not so as Stella would know. As far as she was concerned nothing had changed. Our partnership was doing well, headed for the major league. If we had ended it we could never have told her the real reason why. She had no idea how Charlie felt about her and couldn't have handled it if she had. She was young – only nineteen – when we married, and always had a – a shining innocence about her. Not naivety exactly, just – a sort of inner purity, I suppose. To Stella, Charlie was her big brother, and as such she adored him. She had no idea he was eaten up with jealousy because he knew there was no way he could ever be anything else. Which is what he still can't accept."

"But – in that case, with Stella dead, why are you still partners?"

"Because, when I was . . . out of touch . . . Charlie ran things, and in such a way as to tie us together in what an outsider might regard as a till-death-us-do-part scenario. To untie us now would not only be a very time-consuming business, it would cost an arm and a leg. He would take me for every last cent he could prise loose. Besides, it's much safer to have Charlie inside the tent rather than out, if you know what I mean. Tied the way we are, at least I can see what he's doing. If I couldn't, I would never know when to expect the knife in my back." Luke paused. "I know I can handle him," he said, "if I know you're willing to handle me."

Why not? Fiona thought. She *liked* Luke so much, and together they would make a formidable team. But . . . Always the but, she thought. All right, so we have made very sweet, very passionate, incredibly satisfying love twice; the "but" in this case is that we were both starved: Luke for sex with an emotional context, me for sex, period. But he has always been good to me as well as for me, and I owe him for Aberdeen. Except she knew the last thing he wanted was gratitude and there was no way she could short-change this man. He was worth so much more than that.

"What are you thinking?" Luke prodded.

"About us. How all this has all been so sudden and unexpected. Let's not rush to make any promises or protestations. Let's just take it as it comes and be grateful. Right now we need each other," her smile glimmered, "and as you have probably realised, I'm not cut out to be a nun . . ."

For the first time the clear eyes smiled. "Not with that mouth," he murmured, and kissed it, before drawing her under the covers with him. "I'll take what I can get," he told her seriously. "It's still a hell of a lot more than I've had in a long time."

As they settled comfortably in each other's arms, Fiona could feel his body, wrapped around hers, relaxing into warmth again, while his eventual sigh was that of a man who, knowing he was tired, also knew he would be able to sleep. She felt herself yawn. It's been quite a night, she thought. Closing her eyes, she let her own relaxation take hold before she slid down into the black velvet tunnel of sleep.

Dawn had broken when the butterfly wings of Luke's mouth and the moths of his hands aroused Fiona from her deep, tranquil sleep.

"Let me love you again," he whispered against her lips. "Just so that I know it hasn't all been some marvellous dream . . ."

"I am only too real," Fiona murmured, shifting to allow his lean length to cover hers. "Let me prove it to you . . ."

She did, and again it was her name he said.

*   *   *

117

It was ten fifty when she left Luke's bed with him still sleeping. Fiona deemed it politic to return to her own room before Henry came round at eleven with the morning coffee. On going into the living room to retrieve her robe, she found the room cleared, her kimono gone. It reappeared, exquisitely laundered, in its usual place in her bathroom that night. And while not a word was said she knew that Henry was aware of what had happened because his attitude towards her – always warmly friendly but respectfully polite – underwent a subtle change. A new ingredient had been added. Approval.

Not so from Charlie. He too knew at once – he would have been blind not to pick up the signals which hummed between Luke and Fiona, not to have noticed the thousand and one excuses Luke made to touch her, not to have read the expressive eyes and face or the way he whistled around the place. And the disappearance of the blondes. But he made no comment until a week had passed, every rapturous night of which Fiona had spent in Luke's bed.

She was alone in her office, putting yet another report on disk, when Charlie came in to rifle through the files. When he had found what he wanted he sauntered over to stand in front of her desk. She looked up at him.

"So . . ." he said sardonically, a bite to the smooth voice. "I see the ghosts have been well and truly laid."

Fiona didn't flinch at the taunt, and met his gaze head-on. "You're living up to my expectations again, Charlie. Didn't I tell you I had hoped for more?"

*   *   *

Unable to curb her curious nature, she continued to pick away at the complicated knots which tied two such utterly dissimilar men together. Like why, for a man with a very short length of fuse leading to his patience, it burned awfully slowly where Charlie was concerned. It was as though he was making endless allowances – enough, in Fiona's opinion, to have run up an entire couture collection. But then, the more intimately she got to know Luke, the more she realised that the man she worked with and the man she slept with were but two facets of a multi-faceted character. Unlike Charlie, she and Luke had nothing in common. He was not a man for concerts or galleries or museums. He was an outdoors man who loved horses and took an avid interest in all sport. His volatile disposition had a low flashpoint and he could not abide wasted effort, soon losing interest in anything that was not going to gel. He did not play chess as Charlie did; his games always involved cards and he was a high roller. Yet this man, who coolly bet enormous sums on the turn of a card, and took breathtaking risks with venture capital, was the same man who still occasionally awoke, sweating and shouting, from a nightmare whose terrors Fiona could only begin to assuage.

Charlie might have his depths, but she discovered Luke to be bottomless. He could demonstrate a tenderness that melted, as well as a ruthlessness that chilled. When he knew what he was doing he was unstoppable; when it came to Charlie he was held together with Band-aids. But what had really done for him, Fiona surmised shrewdly, was the fact that he had discovered he was not as invulnerable as he had once believed himself to be. He

had obviously suffered some kind of traumatic break-
down after Stella's death: a trawl through his old files
revealed that he had been out of action for more than a
year, during which time Charlie had indeed all but
soldered them together in perfectly legal ways that would
nevertheless take a lengthy and costly court action to
undo. That Luke had not tried it before was indicative of
just how great a hold Charlie had on him through his
tortured sense of guilt. That he had now begun – carefully and with Fiona's help – to explore ways and means
of undoing that hold made it clear to her just how and
where the balance of power had shifted – in her favour.
Which was probably why they handled each other so
carefully. Both having been through the fire, they were
very careful not to play with matches. Both had been
lonely, both had been afraid, both were still wary. But
they trusted one another. If Luke used Fiona as a
bulwark and she used him as a shield it was the kind
of usage each was prepared to accept.

Nine

When her mother rang one morning to say she would be coming to town for a couple of days to do her Christmas shopping, Fiona was taken aback – for she had not given it a thought – to find how near it was to the festive season, but she took herself across to Onslow Square at the first opportunity with a huge armful of the freshest flowers she could buy, only to find that Maisie, who "kept an eye on things", had already been apprised of Lady Sutherland's impending arrival and, having stocked up the fridge, was in the process of removing dust-sheets and preparing the flat for residence.

When Fiona told Luke he said at once: "She must come to dinner. How about tonight?", but Fiona wanted time to prepare the ground since she knew of old how unerringly her mother could spot a triangle – temporary, eternal or just mere decoration – so she took evasive action by saying: "I don't yet know how she's fixed for invitations, but if I know her, every minute of her time is spoken for."

"How about yours?"

It was casual, but by now Fiona knew what lay beneath it. "My mother needs no looking after," she reassured him.

"Great, because I do. But I would like to return her hospitality. Ask her to lunch, dinner – whatever, but ask her. Tell her it would be a favour to me. Is there anything else I can do for her? Does she need a plane?"

"My mother is old-fashioned. She always has and always will come down from Scotland by the night sleeper. But I'd like to meet her at King's Cross if that's all right with you?"

"Sure . . . Tell you what, bring her back to lunch. I'll tell Henry . . ."

Fiona had no choice but to issue the invitation when she met her mother, who said: "How kind. And I should love to see Luke again, and I shan't be any bother, darling. Far too much to do. I've got a list as long as my arm and invitations from everyone . . ."

She took over the moment she entered the house in The Boltons, looking enchanting in a Cossack fur hat and bearing a brace of grouse, plus – wrapped in sacking in its special ice-box – a Spey salmon which made Henry's eyes gleam. "From the deep freeze," she explained apologetically, "but none the worse for that, since it went in there within half an hour of being landed."

Luke was able to flaunt his previous acquaintance, Charlie was at his smoothest, while Henry was well pleased with his grouse and salmon. In no time she had all three men eating from her hand.

"My dear!" she said urgently to her daughter, when the two of them had a moment alone in Fiona's bedroom after lunch. "You didn't tell me the half of it! I envied you Luke, but where on earth did you come across such a magnificent specimen as that pale-copper Apollo?"

"In the course of a day's work."

"Work! No woman could possibly keep her mind on her work around him!"

"All it takes is a little application."

"Were I thirty years younger I know what *I* would like to apply, but something tells me it would be a waste of time. I made the connection at once, of course – or should I say resemblance?"

Fiona met her mother's knowing eyes as best she could.

"Is that why you didn't mention him when you were home in October?"

"No mountains out of dust-motes, Mummy. Please."

"I doubt if Henry ever allows them to so much as settle. What a cook that man is! I had intended to invite Luke to come up with you for the holidays, but now I see all three must come – which reminds me, Rory has reopened Ballater House and is having a house party this year. Millie Strathcairn seems to be acting as unofficial hostess, while that chinless-wonder husband of hers flutters in the background like a wounded grouse . . ."

Lady Sutherland flitted from one subject to another, but Fiona was well aware that she was being monitored. The fact that her mother had invited the other three-quarters of the household up to Scotland to celebrate Christmas and New Year indicated that she had not only spotted the situation but was intent on exploring it.

Fiona sighed inwardly. It was not what she would have preferred. Luke, yes; that would have been perfect. Luke and Henry would have been lovely. But not Charlie as well. It was too dangerous. It would also be very bad manners to leave him behind. There was just no way she could get out of it without spilling the beans. Hogmanay was *the* family celebration of the year; not to be part of it was unthinkable. She would just have to be on her guard, that was all . . . She had seen the speculation in her mother's eyes, and whilst she was aware that her stock had gone up several points, she also knew she would be expected to come clean as to the possibility of an even bigger investment. The trouble was, even now she was still not sure.

It was snowing when they arrived at Dalcross Airport on Christmas Eve. Fiona's eldest brother, Iain, was waiting for them with the Range-Rover. He had the red hair of the family, but to look at he was nothing like his sister, being a Sutherland and built on the lines of a champion caber-tosser.

"Let's get on our way before this snow really sets in," he said, eyeing the sky. "It's a good hour's drive."

Right on cue, the snow thickened as they drove. "Damn this for a lark," Iain growled. "If it keeps up it'll put paid to the Boxing Day shoot, which will be a great pity as the birds are plentiful this year and I should be able to provide you with a good day's sport. Seeing as you're from the Wild West I needn't ask if you know one end of a gun from another . . ."

Fiona held her breath but Luke's voice was coloured with just the right shade of regret when he answered: "I'll have to take a rain check on that, I'm afraid. I've got a meeting in Aberdeen the day after Christmas."

"Oh, pity . . . How about you, Mr Whitesky?"

"Charlie – and I wouldn't miss it for anything."

"Good, good . . . Henry?"

"I'll be in the kitchen learnin' all about Scots cookin'."

"By all means! My mother tells me you're already a whiz at every other kind."

Fiona was sitting in the front beside her brother, and as much as she might long to she knew better than to turn round and look at Luke, but Henry, ever alert to danger where Luke was concerned, leaned forward to peer out of his window and ask: "Is that stretch of water I can just about see the famous Loch Ness I've heard about – the one with the monster?"

"No, that's the Moray Firth. The loch is not on our way, I'm afraid, but it is near enough to us to be able to take a trip to see it if you really want to."

"Have you ever seen the monster?"

"No, but when I was a boy my father had a gillie who swore he had. However, since he liked his dram there was some doubt as to whether it was the monster or a mistaken pink elephant."

The general laughter had Fiona sighing with relief. Thank you, Henry, she thought. There was no meeting in Aberdeen: she had cleared Luke's calendar for the holidays. But it would get him away from the guns . . .

Lady Sutherland was waiting – somewhat anxiously because of the now-raging blizzard, since it was not unknown for the road through the glen to be blocked if the snow was bad – to welcome them, along with Moira, Iain's wife, and the twins, ten-year-old Jamie and Fergus, who were disappointed to see that Charlie was

125

not wearing either warpaint or feathered bonnet, but too well-mannered to show it.

"Welcome everyone, welcome . . . come in and get warm. There's hot coffee waiting, or a dram if you prefer it . . . Logie will see to your luggage . . ."

Moira dug Fiona in the ribs. "You sly dog . . ." she murmured, eyeing Charlie as she would a particularly luscious pastry. "No wonder you stay in London . . ."

After coffee and shortbread – for which Henry requested the recipe – the guests were shown to their rooms, Moira taking it upon herself to show Charlie to his.

Once in Luke's room: "I'm sorry . . . I should have warned you about the Boxing Day shoot. It's a tradition," Fiona hastened to apologise.

"That's OK."

"Want me to come to Aberdeen with you?" Her warm heart ached at the thought of him all alone there, with God knows what kind of thoughts.

"Your place is here, with your family." It was pleasant, but final.

Damn! thought Fiona. She resolved that after lunch, provided it had stopped snowing, she would take him for a walk, ostensibly to show him round, but really to jack up his obviously deflating spirits. Mentally she kicked herself black and blue for being such a fool as to forget that her brother liked nothing more than a day's shooting, and would naturally expect a couple of Westerners to have been, as he was, raised with guns. But she was impressed with Luke's quick thinking, even though she knew how fast his mind worked. Aberdeen – an oil town of long standing – was the perfect excuse for a man who had never so much as picked up a gun since he had shot his wife's head off.

Better there than here, she told herself. But she still had a sense of foreboding. We shouldn't have come, she thought. Something is telling me we shall regret this . . .

After lunch, when the snow had eased somewhat, Iain pre-empted Fiona's plans by nobbling Luke to ask his advice about some feelers he had received from a company that wanted to build an oil terminal on some land he owned north of Aberdeen.

"Why don't you show Charlie round?" Lady Sutherland asked. "Moira has things to do and I want to have a heart-to-heart with Henry."

"I'd like that," Charlie said easily, and when the twins clamoured to come too, Fiona was only too happy to have them along, making them wrap up warmly in brightly coloured parkas, woolly hats and mittens. She did the same herself, and when Charlie appeared in a bright scarlet padded jacket, Moira sighed *sotto voce*, "Positively consumable."

Wrong, Fiona thought. Charlie's the one who gets to satisfy his appetite.

The twins fell on the snow with cries of glee, pelting each other with snowballs before setting to, with Charlie's help, to build a fat snowman. Fiona found pebbles for eyes and a nose, plus some scarlet holly berries for a mouth, after which she went to the small downstairs cloakroom, ferreted around and came up with a deer-stalker left by some long-ago guest, along with an old tartan muffler. With a pipe of her father's stuck in his mouth the snowman was very lifelike, so naturally the twins had to try and demolish him by pelting him with snowballs. Charlie showed them how to pitch baseball-style, winding up and letting loose, and once they had mastered the art a general free-for-all ensued, the three of them pelting Fiona in a three-pronged attack. There was a great deal of shouting and laughing, and as Fiona fled past the library windows she saw Luke standing at them, watching. She waved, before shrieking as a snowball caught her right in the neck, causing her to take refuge in the forest which edged the drive, losing herself in the trees. It was silent there, only the sough of the wind rustling the pines. She couldn't hear the twins. No doubt they were stalking her. She was creeping carefully forward when suddenly an arm was around her throat and she was held fast against a hard, male body.

"Got you!" Charlie laughed softly.

Fiona held herself very still. "But not where you want me."

"Give me time."

"Not even the time of day."

Fiona's tone of voice made him drop his arm and she moved away. In the darkly green shadow of the trees he was a bright scarlet patch. Fiona was reminded of a cock pheasant. Yes, that was Charlie, all right. All bright plumage and strutting, confident maleness. In her tobacco-brown suede jacket, Fiona felt very much the dowdy little hen.

"We'd better find the twins," she said. "This far north it gets dark early."

"I found you – won't I do?"

Fiona eyed him. "It's what you will do that troubles me."

"Back to that again?"

"We never left it."

"Then let's deal with it once and for all. You lectured me on the virtues of honesty, remember? So how about you admitting the truth of your using Luke as a substitute for me."

"Never!"

Charlie smiled.

"I would never do that to Luke! I am as honest with him as he has always been with me."

"So you have told him about us? About how it is with us? How I know it isn't, and never can be, with him?"

His derisory tone told her he knew she had done no such thing. Reaching out a leisurely hand, he grasped her wrist to draw her helplessly towards him. She pulled back even as every bone in her body liquefied and her heart stumbled. Around Charlie, her body obeyed no summons but his. It was a fatal weakness in her. With Charlie she just could not help herself.

"See . . ." he murmured, reading her every quiver. "Your body says yes . . . It will always say yes to me, no matter how much your mind tells you different. It's never like this with him, is it? Why don't you admit it to yourself? You felt sorry for him and you were afraid of me, of what I do to you – or rather you convinced yourself you were. Pity is all you will ever feel for Luke, and he already has enough of that of his own."

That last sneer saved her. "You should know," she accused. "You made him that way."

"Ah . . ." It was smug with satisfied confirmation. "Given you the sob-story, has he?"

"He told me the truth."

"Maybe – but whose truth?"

"The plain, unvarnished kind. As to how he accidentally killed his wife."

"Not accidentally – deliberately; and not killed – murdered." Charlie's face and voice were seared with contempt. "I wouldn't have thought that you, of all women, would believe his soft-soapy lies." The black eyes burned into her. "What is it about him? The clean-cut, all-American-boy air?" With savage mockery: "How could anyone be so cruel as to believe *he* could kill his wife and make it look like an accident?"

"I don't believe he did!"

"You weren't there. I was! He is as guilty as hell!"

"It was an accident!" Fiona hurled at him. "But you can't forgive him because it was Stella he killed. It always comes back to her and what she meant to you. That is what lies between you; why you won't let him get over it? Well I've got news for you. You will never convince me that Luke is a murderer – never!"

"But that's exactly what he is! He was tired of Stella: she was a hindrance to him once he got his first billion. She was OK for the wife of a rancher-cum-small-time-oilman, but not for J. J. Lucas, one of *Fortune*'s 500! You are the kind of wife he began to want then: breeding, brains and beauty. All he ever had from Stella was the beauty, and a loving heart." Charlie's laugh stripped skin. "And you accuse *me* of being a user!"

"You are – and only for your own ends! You're the

one who flourished me at Luke the minute you realised
he was beginning to regard me as more than just a
damned good PA. You're the one who decided to use
that burgeoning interest to further interests of your own!
Fortunately, I realised what you were up to because I had
been been there, done that and didn't buy the T-shirt!
You profess to have feelings for me, but they are nothing
compared to the jealous hatred you feel for Luke! All I
will ever be to you is a convenient means to a desired end.
Luke has *never* used me like that. (*Except that once*, jibed
her memory). Don't waste your time, Charlie. I will never
believe Luke murdered his wife. I know he couldn't
because—"

"Because what?"

Because in the very act of making love to me he called
me by her name with such love and longing, Fiona
thought, feeling that queer little wrench inside that always came when she remembered that night. No two-
faced murderer could have said that name in such a way.

"Because he still loves her," she said at last. "And
always will."

"Yet he sleeps with you, who has this hang-up about
being used! What else is he doing but using you for sex?"

"It's not like that—"

"From where I stand it's *exactly* like that!

"You don't understand," was all Fiona could say, and
it sounded feeble even to her own ears.

"You're damned right I don't! You have one set of
rules for him and another for me. Why is that – because
I'm only half white?"

Shocked, Fiona stared at him, perceiving for the first

time how thin was the layer of surface assurance which she had mistakenly believed to be bone deep. "You know that's not true," she stated quietly.

"Then why are you so willing to believe what he says while refusing to believe me? Why is it only Luke who has needs and longings?"

"Because you don't have any," Fiona replied, acknowledging a truth even as she spoke it. "But you do *want* revenge. Why? Why can't you leave Luke to find his own absolution? Are you so incapable of comprehending how hard he is finding it to forgive himself that you have to remind him at every turn that what he has done is unforgivable?" Fiona drew a deep breath, firming her voice before continuing: "As for us, I played with fire once before and got badly burned. I won't knowingly go near the flames again."

"Everything worthwhile involves a certain amount of risk."

"Except on your part. Yes, physically you and I set off sparks. Yes, I find you deeply and powerfully attractive, but my instincts keep telling me you're not to be trusted and they doubt if you are either kind or good. Luke is both, and I would trust him with my life. You never do anything unless it suits *you*. It will always be what *you* want. Not so with Luke. Which is why I will never, *ever* do anything to hurt him. Do I make myself clear?"

"You are in love with him!" Charlie's voice shook the snow from the trees. "I take it all back! I thought you ran to him because you couldn't handle me. Now I see you have taken his line: poor, wounded, oblivion-seeking Luke. No danger of going up in flames with him: he is far too cool, far too controlled. I've known him a hell of a sight longer than you have and I know his iron nerve; he's a risk taker – like the risk he took when he murdered Stella. He got away with it because no one would believe that he, of all people, could do such a thing. Only I know better because I know him!"

"It was an accident," shouted Fiona. "She was startled by a rattler."

"Maybe, but she was wearing hide boots – no rattler venom can penetrate that!"

"Than why did she stand up directly in Luke's line of fire?"

"Because he called her name!"

Fiona recoiled.

"Stella knew all about hunting; she'd done it often enough: what to do and what not to, except in a situation like the one he created when he called her name."

Fiona covered her ears with her hands. "Liar!" she screamed at him. "Liar!"

"You can't shut it out, any more than I can. That's why I stick with him: he knows that I know and I intend to see that one of these days he admits it. Only then, when the truth is at last out in the open, will I let Stella's spirit rest."

Fiona turned and ran. Away from Charlie and his corrosive hate and anger, away from her own fear and confusion, away from the terrible knowledge he had just heaped on her; from the consequences it could bring, all it could destroy. Only when she could run no further did she collapse against the rough bark of a pine tree, chest heaving, breath rasping. When she got her breath back she slid down to the ground, her back against the tree, and put her head on her arms. It couldn't be true. It just *couldn't*. Charlie was being his usual, devious self. Luke would never have called his wife's name then, when she stood up, coolly shot her head off. Not the Luke who was so tortured by guilt that he needed Charlie's whip. Not the Luke who had said the name Stella in such a voice, with so much love. There had been nothing of murderous intent there. Only exaltation.

But Charlie had been so right in other things. Luke *was* a risk taker. He did have an ice-cold nerve. But he was so *open*. So honest. And he was no liar. Why would he murder someone he loved so much? Nor could she accept that Stella had not been good enough. No – no, she would never believe that. Stella had been everything to Luke. In losing her he had lost part of himself. Why else the blondes? His wife's hair had been black, like her brother's. *No!* Of one thing she was absolutely certain. Stella still had Luke's heart and always would. He was a one-woman man. Oh, he was as passionate as she could wish, loving enough, tender enough. But she had never kidded herself as to what she mainly represented to Luke: confirmation of his standing as a functioning, perform-ing male. And after all, wasn't she using him as a bulwark against Charlie? All right, so it wasn't love, but it was better than nothing, and since when was one allowed to have everything? Life's rules prohibited that.

She sat there for a long time, until she was shivering, both from cold and reaction, feeling a desperate tiredness rooted in a paralysing sense of doubt. She had been wrong about Rory. Was it possible she was also wrong about Luke? In fact, a lousy judge of men. Whatever, she wasn't up to facing him just yet. Not until she had thought this through.

She got to her feet, and with dragging steps left the woods by a path that came out at the back of the castle, where a small studded door led to the keep. Wearily she climbed the spiral of stone stairs which led to the tower and the little room she had made her special place as a teenager. She had put rugs on the stone floor, cushions on the stone benches, installed a Calor gas heater, arranged books on the shelves, placed warmly shaded oil lamps here and there. Now, she shut the door behind her with a sigh and leaned back against it, emotionally drained. After a few moments she lit the gas heater, its glow brightening as well as warming the cold stone of the little room. Then she lay down on one of the cushion-layered benches and, drawing a Shetland rug over her, wept herself into a miserable sleep.

Luke found her there. She was curled into a ball like a hedgehog, hands tucked under her armpits, for the heater had run out of gas, and her head drooped like a wilted flower. He touched her cheek softly. It was cold. "Fiona."

Her lids fluttered, before lifting to reveal eyes that were like bruises in her pale, tear-stained face. For a long time they looked at each other, then Fiona blurted: "Charlie says you murdered Stella because you wanted rid of her. Did you?"

His eyes never wavered but she saw their clarity darken in the way she knew betokened anger. "No." His voice was flat calm and steady.

"Then why does Charlie believe you did? He made it sound so – so – true. He says you called her name . . . made her stand up so that you could have a clear shot . . ."

"I didn't *call* her name – I shouted it, and *after* I had shot her, not before. It was a reaction not a distraction." Dispassionately: "You don't make unnecessary noise when you've cornered a mountain lion."

"Then what makes him so certain that you called it before?"

"Because that's what he chooses to believe. Remember I told you he was in love with Stella?" Luke paused before continuing: "That love took him over, possessed him utterly, changing him from protective brother to jealous lover. He came to resent anyone she spent time with, became jealous of those she liked, hated those she loved. As she grew older and the boys started coming around he drove them away. With his fists, if he couldn't do it with words. Me, he couldn't drive away, so he settled for hating me instead." Another pause. "What had him tied in knots was the fact that there was no way he could reveal his true feelings for his half-sister. He would really have lost her then, and not just to me. He was also riddled with his own guilt, because what he felt for her is taboo to the Cheyenne. The only way he could handle it was to channel it into jealous hatred of me. I had married her and I had killed her. I had to pay for both."

Luke paused again and Fiona waited. "What Charlie is and what he was brought up to be are two different things. We were raised as brothers, but Charlie is a

136

combustible mix of all that my family, an Ivy League college education and white American culture has made him: well educated, well read, well travelled, with a Harvard Law School degree. He is also a fiercely proud Native American. And it is the latter that he really *is*. He thinks like a Native American, believes like one, such as that Stella's spirit will not rest until she is avenged. But what really drives him is his fear that his own spirit will never know peace in the hereafter, will be condemned to wander until he atones for his – what he regards as incestuous – feelings for his sister, as well as failing to protect her."

"Is that why you keep him around?"

"When my father knew his cancer would kill him, he asked me to look out for Charlie because he told me there was a split in his psyche, and if it wasn't healed he was going to come apart. My father felt responsible, that he had maybe done Charlie a disservice by raising him the way he did, so he asked me to be there for him should the split ever take place."

There was a silence, and for the first time Fiona broke eye contact before she said: "I knew, deep down, that you could never have murdered Stella, not loving her the way you do, but you have to understand that Charlie was so certain sure. You know how he can be . . ."

"Only too well."

"I just – had to hear you say it. I never really believed what he said. I ask you to believe that."

"I do," Luke lied.

"I'm sorry," Fiona said again, and this time her voice cracked. She uncoiled herself, wincing as cramp stabbed her, stood up and began to fold the rug. "What made you look for me here?"

"Your mother. When Charlie came back with the twins he said you'd gone off into the woods on your own, but I know when he's lying." And I was afraid, he told her silently, because I knew he would have been working on you. Now he was confirmed in that view. Charlie had seen the hairline cracks and hammered home the chisel.

Fiona felt stiff with cold and heavy with misery. And a long, long way from Luke. As she headed slowly for the door she didn't see the way he looked after her: the bleakness of his expression, the pain in his eyes. When he said, "Fiona—" she put up a hand.

"No more please, Luke. I can't cope with any more right now. Just – leave me alone to work my way through this. It will be all right. Honestly it will." Her strained voice broke as she wrenched open the door. He heard her feet clatter down the stone staircase and then the thud of the heavy door at the bottom.

After which there was silence.

Ten

On the day of the shoot, Fiona saw Luke's hired BMW disappear round the bend of the drive with a sense of relief tarnished by guilt. She was happy for him to be out of the way of the guns, but also relieved he was out of the way, period, since what lay between them had become a nagging pain, like a bad tooth. It had ached all Christmas Day, spoiling their enjoyment of the festivities, though both had striven to maintain the fiction that all was well, even showing enthusiasm in their respective exchange of presents: a new Patek-Philippe watch for Luke from Fiona, engraved with his name and a date in November special to both of them; a gleaming alligator handbag from Hermès for Fiona from Luke. But as if by mutual consent each had gone to their solitary bed that night.

Once the shooting party had departed, only Fiona, her mother and Henry were left at the castle. The latter had not gone, he said, because (a) he didn't shoot and (b) he'd rather stay home and learn from Mrs Crawford, who had cooked for the Sutherlands for the past thirty years, how to make "some of your famous Scottish dishes." Earlier that morning, while he was helping Lady Sutherland to fill the big, hay-lined wicker baskets with vacuum flasks of hot soup, venison casserole and coffee to go with the game pies, thick sandwiches of cold goose and stuffing, and wedges of various cheeses to accompany the oat-cakes, he and that lady had had a cosy heart-to-heart. Consequently, when Fiona came back from a walk so long it had the dogs flopping in front of the fire with a relieved sigh, she took due note of her daughter's shroud of gloom and despondency but waited until they were having lunch before remonstrating gently: "My dear Fiona, that is cold roast goose you keep on pushing around your plate, not funeral baked meats, yet you are obviously in mourning for someone or something. If you wish me to offer condolences, the least you can do is tell me the name of the deceased."

"Very funny," was Fiona's unsmiling response.

"I'm serious, darling. That pall of gloom you're wearing is a sign of loss if ever I saw one. What – or should I ask whom – have you lost?"

"You have to possess something before you can lose it."

"Well, you certainly seemed to possess something valuable when you arrived here on Christmas Eve."

"It was only a loan. I had to give it back."

"I rather think that what ails you is something you find you cannot give back." Her shrewd violet eyes examined her daughter's curtains-drawn, door-shut face. "Don't do what you did with Rory, darling. You of all people know what happens to feelings that ferment for too long. It is Luke, isn't it? You two have been treating each other with that excess of *politesse* which invariably means daggers drawn. I think we should examine the

body. I'm a great believer in post-mortems. How else is
one to find out the cause of death?"

"A pathologist too?" Fiona observed testily.

"In the thirty-eight years I was married to your father I
conducted my fair share of them." She touched her foot
to the bell set in the carpet by the leg of the dining table,
in response to which the green baize door opened and
Logie entered.

"Coffee in the library, Logie, if you please. And some
brandy, I think. We are in need of a restorative . . ."

In the library, Shona Sutherland sank into the deep
cushions of her favourite chair, placed at one corner of
the roaring driftwood fire, and sighed beatifically. "How
nice. I've had my share of standing around watching
grouse go to their just reward. Thank heavens I'm now at
an age where I can plead it as an excuse."

"What are you after, Mummy?" Fiona asked with true
Scots dourness. "A true confession?"

"Heaven forfend! No . . . What I have in mind is a
general unburdening. The old cliché still holds true, no
matter how much the – what is it Luke calls them? – the
smart-asses? – sneer at them. A trouble shared *is* a
trouble halved. I think you are suffering from an emotional hangover, and I prescribe a dose of catharsis."

Fiona made no response, just sat staring into the fire,
up to which she had drawn her chair as close as she could
without getting burned. Logie brought in the coffee and
the brandy, and when he had gone her mother poured
some of both for each of them before leaning back in her
chair expectantly.

Fiona drank her brandy, sipped at her coffee and then,

in a dull-with-misery voice, began to tell her mother all that had happened, from the moment she had gone to beard the ogre in his lair at The Boltons, down to the confrontation in the tower room. By the time the story was told Lady Sutherland had fitted into the picture those pieces already supplied by Henry and was thus able to see not only where the damage had been done but who had caused it. "A pretty tangle," was her verdict. "Like all people suffering from inflamed emotions, you've not been able to think for the pain." A pause. "But you were right about Charlie. Not mad or even basically bad, but deeply flawed – and definitely dangerous to know. People in the grip of obsessions always are." She eyed her daughter over her coffee cup. "You are quite firm in your resolve not to return to London with Luke?"

"How can I? I doubted him – worse, I let him see that I did. I allowed Charlie to do the very thing I was determined to prevent: hurt Luke by undermining my faith in him."

"Everyone has doubts, but people in love have them by the lorryload."

"But I never expected to doubt Luke! I know how much he loved – loves – Stella. Feeling the way he does even now, there's no way he could have murdered her, so why in God's name did I for one stupid moment allow Charlie to persuade me that he did?"

After a moment: "Jealousy takes many forms, and insecurity is but one of them," Lady Sutherland said.

Fiona transferred her stare from the fire to her mother.

"Of Stella." At her daughter's expression: "Oh yes . . . Somehow or other you have convinced yourself that

Luke is not yet over his wife – and not just because of the tragic way she met her death. You believe that though her physical presence is long gone, emotionally she is very much alive to both men."

"But she is, don't you see? Unalterably so! I am only a means to an end for both of them, and I had enough of that with Rory."

"*Rubbish!*" Lady Sutherland's voice was so sharp that Fiona jumped. "If ever I saw a man in love it is J. J. Lucas. He's been going around like someone who, having won a fortune on the lottery, has discovered he has lost his winning ticket." She shook her head in incredulous exasperation. "Really, Fiona! For a woman with a healthy fund of common sense you seem to have lost it all! But then, love turns even the most intelligent of beings into absolute idiots. Luke is in love with *you*, you goose. Not a ghost – which is another area where you've taken a wrong turning. You're allowing yourself to be haunted by not only your own emotional past but Luke's. The woman he loves is flesh and blood, not a memory and certainly not a ghost. There is no competition between you and a dead woman – only between Luke and Charlie. In this particular case, my dear daughter, you are the prize."

"Only by default," Fiona insisted stubbornly, "and I would rather lose than win that way. It's no use, Mummy. I can't get past Stella. She haunts both of them."

"You mean she haunts you!"

That stilled not only Fiona's tongue but her body, allowing her mother to continue astutely: "It looks to me as if you have been using her as an excuse because you're still afraid to commit yourself to a man. Rory had a profound effect on you, darling; far deeper than you realise, even now. I know how you have struggled to put all the pieces back together again, but it takes longer than you think. Shattered emotions have to knit together as broken bones do, and the plaster for the cast has to be mixed of equal parts of self-confidence, self-respect, spirit, courage and a willingness to trust once more. It is my belief that you were still not ready to take that chance. Not even with Luke. So you used Stella and her memory as your excuse. It takes a great deal of courage to take a second chance. Which is why you're sitting here eaten up with disgust at your own cowardice. What's worrying you is not what you think you did to Luke, but that you think you have lost him."

Fiona's expression had her mother pressing on confidently: "Tell me. This misery that shrouds you. Is it like the misery you knew with Rory?"

"Oh no!" The response was instant and positive. "That was despair of the soul – I could even think of death as preferable to life with him. This is more of an – an ache, a terrible sense of loss . . . I can't sleep, I can't eat, I can't settle to anything. All I seem able to do is mope."

Her mother threw up her hands. "A classic case. Talk about star-crossed lovers!"

Fiona hissed in a sharp breath then let it out slowly. "That's what Charlie said . . . That I was in love with Luke."

"Of course you are. If it's obvious to me it must be like a beacon to him."

"But – I thought it was because of Charlie's constant

144

polishing of Luke's guilt that I felt so – so concerned and protective. Besides, it was Charlie I hungered for—"

"Only physically. Your body was what responded to him. It was your mind, your emotions – the self that is you – which responded to Luke." Lady Sutherland paused before pressing on again. "With Charlie, it was like Rory, wasn't it? Sheer delirium tremens. An all but irresistible, deeply physical attraction? In another word, sex, and that was divorced from love aeons ago. That's the trouble today: most people confuse the one with the other. But that is why you wouldn't allow yourself to surrender to him – a subconscious awareness that you had been there before and got badly mauled. Mind you, I can understand how you felt. Charlie Whitesky is – like Rory – a most remarkable sexual animal, but with those two, all you get is showy stunt-flying. Luke is good for the long haul. After all, it was him you turned to in Aberdeen and he who turned up trumps. It was Luke who warned off Charlie, saw off Rory and told you the *cinéma vérité* truth about Stella – and that must have been hideously painful – while what Charlie gave you was his Technicolor version, all of it out of focus because of his distorting jealousy. Luke is *over* Stella, Fiona, because he is in love with *you*. Why else the Last of the Blondes? He no longer needs them. *But he does need you.* I saw him leave here this morning and he was in flat despair. You gave him back his self-confidence and now he's every bit as miserable as you are, watching it dribble away through the holes Charlie has drilled."

Fiona was twisting her fingers nervously. "But how do I know it's not gratitude he feels—"

Vera Cowie

"*Gratitude!*" Shona Sutherland threw up her hands. "Love has really unhinged you! He believes he's lost you, and with it his own second chance. You two turned to each other because together you are the means of healing long-lasting emotional scars. People love each other for countless reasons, but in my thesis self-recognition plays a large part, the perception in another person of things in your own self. Human beings are basically selfish, after all. You and Luke see in each other two people who can safely be trusted not to inflict in the future more hurt of the kind you suffered in the past. You *love* each other, which is not at all the same as being *in love*. It has to be, else it wouldn't stand up to the attrition of living together. Which is, of course, the real test of loving: living – in every sense of the word – with another human being without becoming repelled, irritated, annoyed, bored, impatient or angered by them, since when you love a person these things are accepted as a part of what they are, and what matters is being with them and sharing their life. Which is what you want to do with Luke, am I right?"

Fiona nodded slowly. "It sort of – sneaked up on me," she confessed, sounding amazed. "I thought love was like it had been with Rory . . . like it was with Charlie . . ."

"No. What you felt for those two had nothing to do with love but everything to do with lust. God knows, sex can be exciting beyond belief, but once the fire is out all you have left is ashes. Neither of those two touched your mind or heart. Only your libido. With Luke, you have it all, don't you?"

Again Fiona nodded, her mind working overtime.

Leaning back in her chair: "I repeat, a classic case," Lady Sutherland pronounced.

"But – why didn't I spot it for myself?" Fiona wanted to know.

"But you did, darling, like I said. Only it was subconsciously. Why else did you not drag Charlie to the nearest bed? I never thought to hear myself say anything good about Rory Ballater but he taught you the difference between the purely physical and the physical combined with the emotional – the spiritual, if you like. That's the trouble nowadays. People have been brainwashed into thinking that without sex there is no love. Rubbish! Everyone is supposed to be so liberated yet they can't hear the sound of their own chains clanking – the ones that bind them to the endless search for sexual fulfilment. Which brings me to another, very salient fact. Not for one moment will I accept that Luke is not a very sexy man."

Fiona blushed. Her mother smiled.

After a while, and on an admiring headshake, Fiona said: "I don't know how you do it, but just so long as you keep on doing it I don't care."

"Experience is the greatest of all teachers – provided you learn its lessons, of course – and I also still have sharp eyes, excellent hearing and a very good memory. The young never seem to realise that the old were once young too. I know what it's like to love a man: the agonies, the ecstasies, the doubts, the delights. Love should be labelled 'Fragile – Handle With Care', so what do we do? We beat it up, pull it apart with 'he loves me, he loves me not' unthinking destructiveness, and then

147

wonder where it went wrong. I've come to the conclusion that what is supposed to confirm our humanity invariably reveals us at our most inhuman."

"Like Charlie."

"He and Rory are as emotionally twisted as my great-grandmother's candlesticks. Ladykillers in the true sense of the word. But they're also to be pitied, since their only capital is their sexual attraction. While it lasts there is no woman they cannot have, but once that attraction runs out . . ." An eloquent shrug. "Luke is not one of them, thank God. What he has to offer is much more valuable and lasting. An understanding heart. Take it, darling. You could do a very great deal worse."

Impulsively Fiona rose from her chair to go to her mother and hug her hard. "Thank you, Mummy. You've done it again. A long talk with you never fails to put things in their proper perspective."

"Didn't I say that post-mortems reveal a great deal? Not least whether it is a case of death or suspended animation. In your case I diagnose concussion – which is why you are both wandering around in a daze. *Tell him*, Fiona. Don't sit and brood about it. Tell Luke exactly how you feel so that he knows he can tell you the same thing." Briskly: "Now, having handed down Sutherland's Law I propose to lay myself down for an hour or two. Tonight will call on all my resources."

"Thank you for putting them at my disposal."

"Giving advice is dangerous, and the mortality rate is high, with a comparable ratio of blame, but I realise that in your present state of mind, my dear daughter, allowances are called for."

When she had gone, Fiona went back to the big chair and curled up in it, seeing so much more clearly now, thanks to her mother's cleaning of her internal computer screen. She is so right, she thought wonderingly, love *is* blind. It renders you unable to see things that are staring you out of countenance. God bless you, Mummy, she thought gratefully. Your catharsis session has indeed shown me just what I have to do.

I love Luke, she admitted, with a great singing of the heart. And when he comes back I'll tell him so. I'll apologise for misjudging him, for letting Charlie's obsession distort my view. Luke could never kill anything or anyone he loved. And he loved Star-that-Shines. For the first time, the little pang which had always accompanied that name did not make itself felt, because thanks to her mother she now understood what had caused it.

The fire crackled, outside snow began to fall, and, finally feeling warm, inside and out, Fiona dozed and fell asleep.

Car headlights flashing through the windows and across her eyes awoke her. "Luke!" she exclaimed, with a joyful leap of the heart. But it was the shooting party, disgorging from the two Range-Rovers. Disappointment had her retreating from the windows. She didn't wish to have to see Charlie, nor was she in the mood for a rehash of the day's triumphs – if any – so she left the library and ran swiftly up to her room, where she put on her heavy suede car coat, drew a warm woollen tam-o'-shanter over her ears, and went out through the garden room. The dogs, having licked clean recently filled bowls, at once came to her, whuffling and barking, eager to accompany her.

"Come on then, you've been in all day."

It was quite dark, although only four o'clock, but she knew every inch of every path, besides which she had the dogs, who always and unerringly found their way home.

Ony one thing had her confidence limping. What if Luke decided to cut his losses and not return to the castle but fly back to London? No, she told herself firmly. That is not his way. Even if he believed their love was dead he would still insist on a death certificate. But she still found herself repeating a mantra as she walked: "Let him come back. Please, God, only let him come back and I'll make it up to him. Please, let him come back so that I may . . . please."

It was ironic, she thought, that only now, when she was frantic at the very thought of losing him, did she understand and appreciate how much he had enriched her life. She visualised the tall, lean figure. So highly strung, so crisply factual and functional, so passionately virile when aroused, so ruthlessly confident when he knew what he was about, so vulnerable where that confidence had been undermined; capable of black moods and rankling torments but also of fundamental kindness and a heart-stopping tenderness. She had always been comfortable with him, liked him from the start, shared his sense of humour, but not realised when that liking had taken the turning which led to love. She had indeed associated love with the flash and filigree of Rory and Charlie. But true love – the way she now knew she loved Luke – was so very much more. "Oh, Luke,"

she sighed longingly at the very thought, "where *are* you?
I want – I need – to tell you that I love you."

Even as she formed the thought she heard his voice
from behind her. Calling her name. Her heart did back-
flips as she whirled to see him, outlined by the bright
starlight of the now-clear sky and the whiteness of the
snow underneath, his long-legged stride carrying him
purposefully towards her. In an instant she was flying
towards him, arms outstretched, the dogs, thinking it was
a game, running with her.

"Luke, oh darling, dearest Luke . . ." She hurled
herself at him, feeling his arms encircle her, heard and
felt his long sigh of relief. "Oh, Luke . . . darling, forgive
me please – for doubting you, for letting Charlie strew
glass between us. I was so wrong to doubt you. *I know
you*. I know you could never have murdered Stella. You
loved her too much . . . the way I love you . . ."

Sounding breathless: "Say again," commanded Luke.

"I love you. I just didn't realise it – or recognise it,
come to that. But I do now. Oh, Luke, I do now . . ."

She felt the tension leave his body as he put her slightly
away from him so as to be able to look down at her face.
In a voice that had her throat thickening: "If only you
knew how I've longed to hear you say that . . ." he said
simply.

Then there was a long silence until at last Luke raised
his head to say: "You taste of fresh air."

"It makes a change from whisky."

He smiled. "But you still smell of roses . . ."

"Joy," she told him radiantly, "sheer, unadulterated
Joy . . ."

He swept her back into his arms. "I've had a hell of a day . . . you never left my thoughts for a single moment . . ."

"My fault, I'd got myself into a tight corner emotionally and Charlie wouldn't let me out. Can I plead temporary insanity by way of being under the influence of love's young dream?"

"I thought it had turned into a nightmare."

"No more of them, my darling. I swear."

"On oath? All that stuff about the evidence you shall give—"

"Yes, Your Honour. I plead guilty to being so deeply involved with John Jeremiah Lucas that I want to make the only restitution possible, which is to spend the rest of my life making it up to him."

"No extenuating circumstances?"

"Well – I would like several other counts to be taken into consideration."

"Such as?"

"Pride, fear, stupidity, lack of faith, wilful blindness and sundry other malfeasances."

"What in God's name are they?"

"Crimes – and I committed them all."

"In that case . . ." Luke bent his head to kiss her again. "I hereby sentence you to life – in the custody of the said J. J. Lucas."

"Oh yes, Your Honour. Thank you, Your Honour."

Arms about each other, they turned to walk back to the castle. "Looks like we both did some hard thinking," Luke said with relief. "I decided there was no way I could let it lie; that I would have to have it out with you even if

you flayed every inch of my skin with that scalpel tongue
of yours. Nothing you could say would be worse than
you telling me you had nothing to say to me ever again.
You mean too much to me to let Charlie win this one."
He stopped dead and looked down at her, pinning her
with those clear, freshwater eyes: "As God is my witness,
Fiona. It was an accident. Yes, I loved Stella, as much as
I was able to love anyone at that time. But what I felt for
her in no way diminishes what I feel for you. What I had
with Stella was my youth; that is gone and so is she, but
because of you I can now put her where she belongs: in
blessed memory."

"I don't want you to forget her, Luke. I was jealous. I
didn't realise it but I loved you and I wanted you to love
me. Now that I know you do I am able to look at Stella
and not resent her or your past together. What matters to
me is that I am a necessary part of your future."

"Oh, my love . . ." Luke said, in a shaken voice.

After a while they resumed walking again, then he
said: "Thank God you decided to make it personal when
you came to see me that day. Turns out you were
everything I was looking for – in more ways than one."

"I had to be shown the truth of you by someone so
much wiser than me."

"Your mother?"

"How did you guess?"

"Who else fits the description?"

She smiled up at him, and the smile was in her voice
when she said: "In this girl's case, her best friend really is
her mother . . ."

Eleven

That evening, dressing for the ball that always followed the shoot, Fiona was pinning Luke's diamond rose – he had returned it to her once he knew she would wear it, and with pride – to the pleated bodice of her smoke-grey organza dress, above which her hair glowed like oloroso sherry, when her mother knocked and came in.

"No need to ask if you took my advice," Lady Sutherland smiled. "In the course of one afternoon you've run the gamut of rags to riches."

"How do these riches grab you?"

"It's where they will grab Luke that counts – and I will not be so indelicate as to name the parts." Embracing her daughter lovingly; "I am *so* happy to see you out of mourning, darling."

"Oh, Mummy, I didn't know it was possible to be so happy."

"You do seem to be giving off sparks."

Which Charlie had also noticed, because later that evening, standing with his hostess on the edge of the dance floor, watching Fiona and Luke ostensibly dancing but in reality just drifting on cloud nine, he commented sardonically: "Ain't love grand."

"They do make a handsome couple, don't they?"

"Fiona is a beautiful lady."

"And Luke is a very attractive man." With seemingly innocent pride: "I approve wholeheartedly. My daughter has at last found the right man. Her first husband was a wholly unprincipled and selfish wrong man."

"It so happens he was on the shoot today."

"Everyone in the glen turns up," Lady Sutherland told him imperturbably. "It's a long-held tradition."

"He's a good shot."

Lady Sutherland turned to look up at him. "Deadly," she agreed.

Fiona was thirstily downing champagne when Charlie, moving in his usual silent way, materialised beside her.

"May I have the pleasure?" he asked, in a way that had her eyeing him before agreeing airily: "Why not?" Her strength was as the strength of ten because her love was J. J. Lucas.

He led her on to the dance floor: "So, you've made your choice," he opened.

"No. There never was a choice, really. It was always Luke. I just didn't realise it." She paused before sliding in the knife. "Probably because you were doing your damnedest to prevent me. That little episode is now is over and done with, Charlie. Take the necessary steps. Preferably away from us."

"Taking over already? Your ex told me today you have a propensity to do that."

Fiona knew enough not to show her dismay or shock that Charlie and Rory should have gone so far in so short a time. Rory had not been near the glen since the divorce because immediately afterwards, being liable for its costs as well as a lot of other things, he had gone abroad to escape his creditors. True, he had recently reopened Ballater House (and she would dearly love to know what had brought that about), but the fact that he would not only show up on an occasion where almost all of the people present were, unlike him, old and good friends of the host, but also get together with the only other man who had done her wrong, sounded a clear warning. So she kept her tone coolly indifferent when she replied, "He would know. We had many a battle."

"Almost wiped you out, didn't he?"

So . . . They had discussed her. And Charlie was making sure she knew. She told herself that it was only to be expected. Like always gravitated to like. "Which is why I wouldn't let you repeat the exercise," she informed him pithily.

"He told me you had a vivid imagination."

"What I went through with Rory is beyond imagining." Sweetly malicious: "You remind me of him *so* much."

Charlie chose to take that at its face value. "Thank you. He's a good-looking guy." Pause. Then he struck. "He told me he had seen you in Aberdeen with Luke." Another almost 'to term' pause. "I don't think he liked it."

"What Rory likes or does not like has not mattered to me for a long time."

"Well, you still matter to him."

"Only because he's a bad loser. He and I are history, as

you would say." Disengaging herself from his embrace, Fiona stepped back so as to face him, in full attack mode. "All right, Charlie. Now we know where we stand. Let battle commence."

His smile was unfazed. "You know your American history. Indians never fought at night."

"No, but they made plans for the coming day and donned their warpaint."

This time the smile was genuine. "I always liked that about you. Your knowledgeable interest in my people."

"But you won't let that liking stand in your way."

"I never let anything stand in my way."

For a long moment they held each other's gaze, then Fiona turned on her heel and walked away.

Luke was dancing with Lady Sutherland.

"I'll say this for you Scots; you certainly know how to throw a party," he complimented her.

"Wait until Hogmanay – that's when we *really* celebrate. And speaking of celebrations, may I say how happy I am for you both. Welcome to the clan, Luke."

On a grin: "You've noticed, then."

"If we were to switch off every lamp you two would still light up the room."

"They went out for a while," he admitted.

"Only because Charlie was tinkering with the fuses."

Some time later, aglow and breathless from a boisterous reel, Fiona came up to Luke and panted: "Heavens, I must be getting old. Give me a glass of that champagne if you please."

She drained it at a gulp.

"Hey, take it easy. That stuff can go straight to your head."

"True – but not as fast as you do." Her eyes, pure amethyst, sparkled up at him.

"Don't tempt me."

"Why not?"

"You are high!"

"As a kite." She leaned towards him to murmur throatily: "Fly me."

Setting down her glass, he took her by the hand to pull her over to one of the big window embrasures, where behind heavy velvet curtains he proceeded to do just that. They were lost to everything but each other when Henry's voice warned: "I think you two ought to know that a Mr Rory Ballater just walked in."

Luke looked at Fiona, who said, "Not by invitation," in a voice that this time held no fear.

"I owe that son of a bitch for Aberdeen," Luke said, happy not only to pay his debt but in the knowledge that this time Fiona would insist on it.

"He's carryin' a snootful," Henry advised.

"Rory!" Fiona demolished that illusion. "That will be the day! He has a head like a cannonball. If he's acting the drunk then you can bet your bottom dollar he's as sober as a benchful of judges." Which confirmed her suspicions. "He's up to something."

"Let's go and see what it is, then," Luke decided.

Emerging from behind the curtains, Fiona saw that Rory had positioned himself about two-thirds of the way down the great two-storey hall where the dancing was taking place, right in front of the panelled wall where hung the Sutherland collection of ancestral *claidhemh mor* and well away from the whoops, bagpipe skirls and stamping feet of the dancers who were enjoying a vigorous strathspey at the far end. He looked very big and very splendid in full Highland rig, but his voice was overloud, his stance that of a man who has had several drams too many, his handsome face flushed, the blue eyes seemingly unfocused. On his arm was the twenty-years-younger wife of the Laird of Strathcairn, while on his other side stood the laird himself, a chinless wonder who looked as if he would rather be elsewhere, even if he and his wife had both received an invitation. Which Rory had shamelessly used.

"Right, what's your take on the situation?" Luke asked, taking Fiona in his arms again and keeping his back to Rory, with Fiona able to see everything over his shoulder.

"It's as I said. He is no more drunk than I am, and I know that expression. It's what I used to call his 'spoiler' look. I think he's been told all about our relationship, doesn't like it and has come to see what he can do to ruin it."

Her eyes met Luke's and she read in them what she had not said. A certain name.

"Well I'm not about to let anybody spoil anything," Luke said, in a voice that meant business, "not us or your mother's marvellous party. Nor do I want her or you to be the subject of scandal in the glen, so let's ignore him and see if we can't bring him down to us and away from that reeling mob. See what he wants. If it's trouble, there'll still be enough noise going on to cover any rumpus we might make."

He began to kiss Fiona again, the two of them seemingly oblivious to everything but each other, he ostensibly murmuring sweet nothings in her ear but in reality giving her instructions. "OK – if and when he comes down to us I want you to grab his attention. Use that tongue of yours to draw blood. I don't want him watching me, OK? Now, what's he doing?"

"Glaring at us. He's not used to being ignored. I think he's expecting us to confront him; he is here without invitation after all."

"Good. Tell me if and when he comes our way . . ." Luke proceeded to kiss Fiona again, in a way that had her struggling to keep her mind on the job, only to be rewarded when she saw Rory, the clinging arm of Millie Strathcairn notwithstanding, begin to walk towards them. "He's coming," she said against Luke's lips.

"Right. Get ready . . ."

Luke didn't turn. He was giving an excellent impression of a man who not only didn't know that Rory Ballater was there, but didn't care either. Then the well-remembered voice – seemingly a little more blurred than before – drawled, "Well, well, well . . . so my eyes do not deceive me – more's the pity." His eyes raked Luke from head to toe. "How easily some men are satisfied. But then, we know better than to expect good taste from the country that invented the Big Mac. You will forgive me if I dispense with the usual good wishes. It is against my principles to congratulate the man who intends to marry my wife."

Appalled at the way Charlie was leaking privileged information, Fiona still managed to say, in the voice of one truly surprised: "Principles, Rory? I never knew you had any principles. You never did when we were married."

In the face of the sudden crackle of blatant hatred, Millie Strathcairn withdrew her arm from Rory's and took a step backwards, almost treading on her nervous husband's toes. Rory didn't notice, since his attention had become welded to his former wife.

"I know what you were up to in Aberdeen," he sneered. "Taken to fouling your own nest, have you, after fouling so many others?"

"When it comes to playing foul I learned from the master. Nobody does it like you, Rory."

The blue eyes blasted her with ten thousand volts. "Bitch!" he snarled, followed by "Whore!" Which was when Luke moved, so fast nobody could afterwards remember seeing anything, just Rory doubling up as Luke's locked left fist slammed him right at the point where his velvet jacket buttoned and his ribcage curved, causing him to double forward with an explosive "*Ooof!*", thus proffering his chin, whose point Luke clipped hard with his other fist, knocking Rory's head up with such force that he was lifted off his feet, falling backwards to hit the highly polished parquet floor with a thump before sliding along it to meet the panelled wall, hard enough to make the ancestral portraits sway alarmingly. Millie Strathcairn squealed, and her husband blanched, but before anyone else could notice, Henry had materialised to seize Rory by the feet and drag him away into the corner behind a large flower display, where he bent down to lift one of his eyelids. "Out cold," he said in satisfaction. Then, to Luke: "I'm glad to see you remember what I learned you."

"Henry, you're a diamond!" Fiona exclaimed. "And as for you . . ." She turned to Luke. "He never knew what hit him! Or who, come to that." Picking up his hands, she put her mouth to the reddened knuckles. "You have just paid *all* my debts," she told him in a voice that raised the hair on the back of his neck. "Now let me show you my gratitude."

Turning to Millie, who had fluttered in hand-wringing mode to kneel by the once-mighty fallen, she ordered grandly: "Dispose of the remains. Cremation, perhaps?" before bearing Luke away in the direction of the stairs.

From where he stood, all but hidden behind a massive Georgian wing-chair placed by one of the two enormous fireplaces that warmed the hall, Charlie watched them go.

Nobody else had noticed a thing.

A little while later Lady Sutherland approached Henry to ask: "Where are Luke and Fiona? I haven't set eyes on them for the past half-hour."

"Probably billin' and cooin' somewhere," Henry told her with diplomatic truth. "You know how lovers is . . . They'll be back directly . . ."

In the library, holding an ice-packed towel to his aching jaw, Rory Ballater listened as Charlie Whitesky talked. Outside the closed door Millie Strathcairn pouted affrontedly, while her husband fiddled with the lace at his neck and wished to God he had never set eyes on Rory Ballater. When finally the two men came back into the hall Millie saw with immense relief that Rory's mood had changed for the better, but she knew that smile. It boded ill for somebody – probably the American who had so unexpectedly floored him. She glanced curiously at the other American but he disappeared back into the mêlée without a word.

"Come on," Rory ordered. "We're leaving. Nothing to stay for now . . ."

When Lady Sutherland set eyes on her daughter and her lover again, they were dancing close and dreamily.

"See . . . what did I tell you," Henry said.

Fiona slept late next morning, as did most people, since the ball had not ended until 4 a.m. It was lunchtime before she surfaced, only to find that Luke had flown to London by the early plane.

"What on earth for?" she asked Henry, both miffed and mystified. "He never said a word to me."

"He'll be back tonight," Henry reassured. "Told me to be sure and tell you. Something important he had to do, he said."

"Oh, well, I have things to do myself," Fiona said, inventing a trip to the village where, as luck would have it, she ran smack into Rory as she was leaving the post office. He had a swollen lip and a badly bruised jaw.

"Why, Rory! I've never seen you looking better," Fiona exclaimed happily. Once she would have cowered before the look he directed her way; now she sent it back in spades. "Lay so much as a finger on me and I'll set

Luke on to you." Her smile stripped skin. "You know what he can do by now." Her deadly dispassionate eyes measured him from head to toe with slow deliberation, making his scowl deepen.

"And to think I once went in fear of you."

Turning on her heel, she stalked away.

Had she seen the way he looked after her she would have taken to her heels, and had she also seen whom he met in the bar of the Sutherland Arms five minutes later she would have warned Luke when he returned that night, in time for dinner.

"Why didn't you say you were going to town? I would have come with you."

"Something I needed to do."

"Like what?"

"If you'll walk this way I'll show you."

He led her into her father's study, shutting the door on them. "Close your eyes and hold out your hands."

She did so and felt him place a velvet-covered box into them. "More presents?"

"Look inside and see."

Doing as she was told, she exposed a magnificent ten-carat, rose-diamond solitaire. When she found her voice: "Is this a reward for being a good girl?" she asked.

"It's for being *my* girl, or do you still say fiancée over here? Do you want to try it on for size?"

Somewhat shyly, Fiona held out her left hand and Luke slid the ring down the third finger. It fitted perfectly. "There you go. Now it's all official. How about we seal the bargain?"

"With a kiss?"

"I had something a little more comprehensive in mind . . ."

Later, she held up her hand to splay its fingers wide, turning her hand this way and that, causing the magnificent jewel to splinter into shards of dazzling, flashing light. "Now I understand how Elizabeth Taylor feels! I know you're a veritable Rock of Gibraltar, my love, but you didn't have to go and buy it for me – and how did you know my ring size anyway?"

"Your mother . . ."

"Why, that sly old puss! She never said a word . . ."

"That's because I asked her not to. I took a ring of yours with me to show the man at Cartier. I also bought two wedding rings. I want us to be married as soon as possible."

"How soon?"

"Well, me being an American, there seem to be certain residential complications and qualifications if we do things your way, so I thought we'd do it mine."

"What do you mean?"

"You'll find out all in good time . . . That's something else I had to do today . . ." Which was all he would say.

The engagement was announced at dinner, the ring being displayed to great admiration. Toasts were drunk, approbation, congratulations and champagne flowed. Lady Sutherland was proudly contented, Iain was forthright in his approval – "Luke is ten thousand times the man that other shit was" – while Moira added succinctly: "Iain is right, you know. It's about time you had a man who takes such pleasure in giving after a man who knew only how to take."

Charlie said only a sardonic "Diamonds really are a girl's best friend, then." Fiona smiled pityingly. "Not when you have a mother like mine."

The official announcement was made at Hogmanay, at which festivities Rory Ballater was conspicuous by his absence.

Twelve

They returned to London in the new year, and it was then that Fiona found out what Luke had meant by doing things his way. It meant being married in the American Embassy – officially designated American soil – and by the round-faced, smiling judge, who happened to be back in London attending some international legal convention.

Judge Mennenger – for that was his name – was only too happy to officiate, and told Fiona so when they got together so that he could take her through the legal formalities.

"I don't mind telling you I had high hopes of something like this when I met you at Thanksgiving. I could see then that Luke was more than a mite smitten. In my opinion – and it is not a legal one – you are the best thing that has happened to him in a long time."

"You mean since Stella's death."

"Yes. I'm sure Luke can now put that whole sad episode behind him. Charlie too . . ." He took off his glasses, began to polish them with a brightly coloured silk handkerchief. "Luke tells me you know a lot about Native Americans."

"Only what I've read. Charlie is the first one I've met.

I'm sure you know much more than I do, but—" Fiona hesitated.

"Ask away," encouraged the judge.

"Well ... what has always interested me is their spiritual tenets, such as their belief in spiritual magic, with all its signs and portents. I've read that it plays a large part in their religion, especially vision quests."

"You know about them?"

"Not as much as I'd like to. Only that they have special lodges where they go with their own, individual medicine bundle in order to enter a state of altered consciousness, and that in that state they experience visions enabling them to commune with the spirits of the dead, through which they gain insight into personal difficulties and emotional problems."

"That's exactly how it is. Vision quests are an inextricable part of Native American culture, and a very important one. They find their way forward through them. The Cheyenne half of Charlie fervently believes in their power. So did my mother, and she was only one-quarter Cherokee."

"And don't they also believe that if you give a child the name of a much loved but now dead person, the qualities that person possessed will be transferred to the child along with the name?"

The judge smiled. "I see Luke was right. You do know about Native Americans."

Fiona was silent awhile, then asked: "What was Stella like – to look at and as a person?"

"Small, dark, graceful, very pretty. Sweet-natured.

Always believed the best of people. Not a spiteful bone in her body."

"How old was she when she died?"

"Well now, let me see . . . She was nineteen when she married Luke and they were married seven years, so she was twenty-six when she died, five years ago now."

Of course, Fiona recalled. We were of an age when we married; but at twenty-six I was divorced, while she was dead . . . "And there were never any children?"

"Not for want of trying. Stella lost three babies in the first five years because she had the type of high blood pressure which makes pregnancy both dangerous and difficult. She knew it but she was determined to give Luke the children he wanted if she could. When it became certain that she couldn't they talked about adoption, but she died before anything got started." The judge patted Fiona's hand. "I'm sure he and you will have as many children as you want. It does me good to see what you've done for and to him already. He's happy for the first time in a long time, and after what he went through he needs all the happiness he can get."

While Luke liaised with the embassy regarding the wedding ceremony, Fiona busied herself with the sale of her flat and the agency. Her life with Luke would take her wherever he went, which meant that she had no use for the one and no desire to run the other long-distance. Fortunately Sue Ryland, her assistant, had always coveted Crème de la Crème, and once she knew it was to be sold immediately made Fiona an offer she could not refuse. The lease of the flat in Cornwall Gardens had been bought by Rory's mother as a wedding present, and had been part – actually the only part, because Rory was fathoms deep in debt – of her divorce settlement.

Her first inclination at the time had been to sell it, but her father had advised her to hang on to it as an investment, while her mother – as always practicality personified – had pointed out that it was ridiculous to pay rent elsewhere when all she had to do was redecorate and refurnish to turn it into something completely new. So she had done just that, getting rid of everything that had anything to do with Rory before making it over into something that in no way resembled what it had been before. Only then was she able to live there, and had done so quite happily. She had not sub-let it on taking up residence in The Boltons, since she didn't need the money, and besides she didn't like the idea of strangers living in her house and handling her private possessions; but now she put it in the hands of an estate agent without a second thought, and what with meetings with him, the judge, her lawyers and her bank manager, discussions with her mother as to a guest list, fittings for "the perfect wedding dress" and consultations with various other people involved in the ending of one life and the beginning of another, she was so busy that when the estate agent called to say he had a firm offer at her asking price for the remainder of her lease but that the offer was conditional on early occupation, she had no choice but to leave her wedding preparations in order to go across to Cornwall Gardens and make a start on readying it for vacant possession.

It was a raw January afternoon and the flat was chilly,

smelled musty and looked unlived-in – not surprising, since it was months now since she had done so. Switching the central heating to high, she also turned on the gas logs in the living room and sat on the floor in front of their heat to sort through drawers and boxes, putting into one pile what was disposable, and into another, smaller pile, what was not.

The Louis Vuitton alligator dressing case that her been her twenty-first-birthday present from her mother she would take with her, along with the lovely old T'ang horse and the exquisite Ming vase, both of which she had been left by her grandmother Fraser, all that was left of her treasured heirlooms, for Rory had sold the Raeburn, the Georgian tea- and coffee-pots and the complete set of Baccarat crystal stemware. She packed her hi-fi system and CDs, all her books and the family photographs, in albums since Rory had sold their original silver frames. Her jewellery had gone very early on to pay gambling debts, and everything else connected with him and/or her marriage she had discarded at the time of her divorce. But she still sifted carefully through each drawer and cupboard in case anything had been overlooked, having no desire to take into her new life anything that had the slightest connection with the bad parts of the old.

When she heard the key in the lock she looked up in surprise. The only other person with a key to the flat was her mother, and Fiona knew that she and Henry – who had settled into the perfect working partnership – had set this day aside to devote to caterers and florists. Perhaps they had got through their business in record time. But it was Rory who sauntered into the room, a front-door key swinging negligently from one forefinger. One look at his face and Fiona was on her feet.

"What are you doing here? And how did you know I was? More to the point, where did you get that door key?"

His smile was amused, but the blue eyes, she noted, were not. "Come now, my dear Fiona. I know that memory of yours is selective, to say the least, but do I have to remind you that I did once live here? The key is my own. How fortunate that the only thing you left unchanged in your makeover was the lock on the front door . . . Even more fortunate is the fact that it should come in so handy at this particular time . . ." He glanced around at the heaped piles. "Clearing out again, I see . . . Getting rid of everything the way you got rid of me?" He tutted reprovingly. "You should know by now that I never let go of anything until I'm good and ready to release it. I suppose you can't wait to set sail on that sea of oil your Yankee lover owns. Landed the big one this time, haven't you? I've made some enquiries about Mr J. J. Lucas. Seems he owns half the state of Oklahoma, not to mention large swathes of Wyoming, where his wells produce enough oil to float the Isle of Wight. You certainly know how to pick 'em."

Fiona's unruly tongue counter-attacked. "Then how come I picked you?"

In an almost leisurely fashion, his hand met her face in a blow which nevertheless sent her staggering backwards, and also indicated what she was in for. "Watch your tongue!"

She put up a suddenly trembling hand to her swelling

cheek, sliding a glance at the open door and wondering if she could make a dash for it. "You can't treat me as your property any more," she reminded him. "I am no longer without a protector. You of all people know by now what Luke is capable of."

This time he backhanded her with such force that she fell to the floor.

"I know all about your so-called fiancé. In fact, I know a great deal more than you think."

"Charlie," Fiona said flatly, even though it hurt to speak.

"Smart chap – for a Red Indian."

"The political correctness police insist they be referred to as Native Americans nowadays. Your prejudices are showing, Rory."

"They're not all I intend to show you."

Fiona's heart lurched but she managed to say steadily: "Don't be more of a fool than you already are. Whatever you have in mind, Luke will see that you pay for it. As you pointed out, he is a rich and powerful man."

"I have merely come to pay my debts," Rory denied virtuously. "And I owe you for so very much, my dear Fiona."

"True . . . it was always my money you used."

One hand snaked forward to drag her up to face him, the other swung viciously both ways, driving her teeth through her lip.

Sagging in his grip: "Once he knows what you've done, Luke will make it a police matter," she mumbled through split lips. "You won't get away with beating me this time."

175

"Oh, I know all about his clever ways with the police – the American kind in particular. Has them in his pocket, of course. God knows it's deep enough. Actually managed to murder his wife and get away with it. I may have had to . . . discipline you from time to time, but I never went as far as murder."

As she opened her mouth to try a scream his hand went round her throat, fingers biting deeply into her flesh. "One sound and it will be your last."

But her valiant Scots spirit would not be quelled. "You've been watching too many late-night movies. Even your dialogue is old hat."

His long fingers increased their pressure and dots danced in front of her eyes. "What I have in mind needs no dialogue. And didn't I always tell you that actions speak far louder than words? I doubt if our colonial cousin will take kindly to a battered bride. Americans set such great store by 'good-looking broads', don't they?"

Which was when she knew he was here to do to her what Luke had done to him. Demolish her. Violence had always been his way of settling scores. In desperation she tried to knee him, but he only moved out of range, his laugh a taunt. She kicked, she scratched, she tried to gouge, all to no avail. He was so much bigger and stronger than she was, besides knowing from experience just how and where to hurt her so that all the strength she had ebbed away in gasps of pain. Long before the beating was over she was limp in his hold, no longer conscious of anything.

When she came to it was dark and cold and she was alone, hurting dreadfully all over. He had spitefully turned off lights, fire and central heating, and she was shivering convulsively. It hurt to breathe, but it was the other, deeper pain in her abdomen which brought sweat to her brow and terror to her heart. Rory's blows had ruptured something. Oh God, she thought desperately, oh God, no . . . I must get help. She set herself to crawl towards the telephone, but it was slow and agonising; she had to keep stopping to regain strength. As she did so she left a trail of blood behind her. She was still a foot away from her desk, where the phone sat, when she heard the front door open again and terror stilled her. He'd come back to finish her off . . . Gritting her teeth against the pain, she curled herself into a foetal ball, but at the first touch of a hand she knew whose it was.

"Come to gloat, Charlie?" she croaked, as he carefully raised her up, causing her to cry: "Oh, don't . . . ! I think something's ruptured inside . . . I'm bleeding . . ."

Through blurred eyes she looked up into a face that was more impassive than she had ever seen it. It was as if his soul had gone into hiding, so veiled was his expression. "Ah . . . Charlie . . ." she panted shallowly, "this is your revenge, remember? We are the ones supposed to suffer . . ." She cried out again as he moved her legs, pain rolling her over the edge into blackness.

When she came to awareness again it was to find he had covered her with a quilt and was bathing her face with amazing gentleness, washing away the blood oozing from the cuts, cleaning the grazes. "The ambulance is on its way," he said, in a voice as opaque as his eyes.

"You're defeating your purpose, Charlie . . ." she croaked. "I never knew you were a Contrary." This was a specialised group within the Cheyenne tribe which had insisted on doing everything in reverse.

"I'm not. But you're losing your child."

"Ah . . . no . . . !" It was a high, despairing wail of agony, and she turned her face away, unwilling to let him see her grief. Which was when she became aware of the towel wadded between her thighs, the stickiness of it. The sound of her breathing was harsh and shallow, and the face he continuously wiped was paper-white and glazed with perspiration. She tried to evade his hand but the movement stabbed her with pain and she clutched at it involuntarily. He let her grip it and squeeze hard when the pain came in like the tide. "Do you realise what you've done, Charlie?" she panted, when it receded. "Between you, you and Rory have murdered Luke's child. It might have been another Stella. Did you ever think of that? Native Americans believe that you can transfer special qualities along with a name, so I thought that's what I would do if and when Luke and I had a daughter. Nobody has ever said a bad thing about Stella, only that she was beautiful, inside and out; as lovely as her name . . . Star-that-Shines . . ." She forced herself to continue speaking though the effort exhausted her. She had to make him understand. "I know you loved her, Charlie, but what matters is that *she loved Luke*. Enough to marry him, to try and have his children, time and again, though she knew she might die in the attempt. That is true love, Charlie. Which is what you're not big enough to accept. *That Stella loved Luke*. Because you wanted her to love you. It was jealous spite made you feed Rory your poison . . . get him all worked up so he could think of nothing but repaying me for divorcing him, Luke for putting him down in Scotland and both of us for having the temerity to love each other. Only you didn't expect him to do this, did you? Never thought he'd go this far ... I could have told you he would, but I wasn't supposed to know what you were up to, was I?"

From then on she slid in and out of consciousness, sometimes recognising him, sometimes not, but always rambling in an increasingly thread-like voice. Then she was talking to Rory: "Never wanted children, did you, Rory? ... Made me have an abortion the first time then beat me up so badly I lost the second one ... Now you've done it again, only this time it wasn't yours, thank God. I never wanted *your* children ... *But I want this baby because it is Luke's* ... Please ... don't let it die ..."

Then she said, in a voice almost normal in its ringing clarity: "You're a cigar-store Indian, Charlie. Made of painted wood. You have no right to call yourself a Human Being because you have no humanity. No Human Being could have done what you have done. Stella would disown you as her brother if she knew ... because you did it in her name, didn't you? Which you have dishonoured. You believe in the spirits, don't you? What must Stella's spirit be thinking of you now ... ?" Then she became incoherent again, pleading and crying for somebody, anybody, to save her baby. When the ambulance arrived a few moments later she was unconscious.

After that everything was very confused. People kept doing things to her; she hurt all over and there was a tube

179

up her nose and down her throat, another in her arm, and a third on a finger. It hurt to breathe and her stomach was sore. But she still struggled to say: "My baby . . . please save my baby . . ." before the darkness rose up to engulf her once more.

When she came out of it she found she had somehow left her body and was floating above her bed. Looking down, she could see herself, her multi-coloured, swollen face unrecognisable with its livid cuts and contusions, her body surrounded by and connected to various machines which beeped continuously, including one which looked as if it was dripping blood. Then she saw that Luke was sitting by her bed, chin on hands that were clasped as though in prayer, eyes fixed to her face. She called his name. He didn't hear. She called it again, louder, but he still did not react. So she went down to him, which was when she saw the tears dripping from his chin on to his hands, and that the clarity of his remarkable eyes was dark with the dullness of despair. When she said his name a third time and he didn't respond she knew the only way she could get him to hear her was to go back inside herself and speak from there. So she did, and when she opened her eyes again she was looking up at him. "Luke . . ." she managed to say in a voice that floated from her as a mere breath. But it was enough to turn the dark eyes to mega-watt brilliance as he exclaimed, "Fiona! Oh, thank God!" before going down on his knees to put his face down on the pillow next to hers.

Her hand was very heavy, but she managed to lift it, touch the thick, tousled blond hair and say, hardly moving her swollen lips: "Don't cry, my love . . . please

. . . I'll be all right now . . ." before losing consciousness again.

It was bright daylight when she awoke, no longer feeling so muzzy but aching all over. The tube was gone from her nose, but not from her arm. Her ribs felt tight and her stomach was still painful. It was very quiet but someone was breathing heavily. Turning her head on the pillow she saw Luke, still in the same chair, but this time fast asleep. He was unshaven, grey with fatigue, head back against a pillow, knees covered with a rug, but one of his hands was so entwined with one of hers that her slightest move would wake him. She lay still and looked her fill until her heavy eyelids refused to stay open and she drifted off into a deep, healing sleep.

She was clear-headed when she next awoke, this time to the warmth of lamplight, to find her mother had replaced Luke, drinking a cup of tea and leafing through a copy of *Vogue*.

"At your devotions?" Fiona murmured, sounding like a rusty hinge.

"Darling!" Her mother was on her feet at once, face and voice ringing a peal of gladness, bending over to examine her daughter's face with anxious eyes, smiling with relief when she saw not only recognition but awareness. "Thank God! You're back with us again! How do you feel?"

"Like I've been trampled by a herd of elephants. My ribs hurt . . ."

"That's because they're strapped. Three of them were fractured."

"I remember tubes and bottles."

"All but one gone now . . . You lost a lot of blood."

Fiona held her mother's concerned eyes. "Besides what else?"

"Your child," was the compassionately honest answer. "They tried, but they couldn't stop the haemorrhaging. Too much damage had been done . . . I'm so sorry, darling." She took her daughter's hands, wrapped them in her own.

"Does Luke know?"

"Of course. You're his overriding concern. He sat by you for three whole days and nights while you were on the danger list. Absolutely refused to leave your side."

"I know . . . I saw him . . ."

"Yes, he told me you'd come round briefly and re-cognised him. I never saw a man so transformed, but it meant we were able to persuade him to get some proper sleep. We were so very worried, darling. You've been through a terrible ordeal. Now we have to help you get well again."

"How long have I been here?"

"This is the fourth day."

Four days! "And where am I?"

"In your own suite at the Wellington. They removed you from intensive care yesterday, satisfied that you're on the mend. Luke was all for flying in every consultant in the business, but they know what they're doing here and saved your life, even if they couldn't save the pregnancy."

"How long have you been here?"

"Since the night you were brought here. Luke arranged for a plane to fly me down. He's been so kind to me, even in the midst of his own terrible torment. I can see why you love him."

"And who told him about what had happened?"

"Why Charlie, of course! Don't you remember him finding you? Thank God he did. If he hadn't, you'd have bled to death."

After a moment: "And Rory? You know it was Rory who did this?"

Her mother nodded, grim-faced. "The police are looking for him right now. After what Charlie told them I hope they throw him in solitary confinement and then forget where his cell is."

"What did Charlie tell them?"

"All that you managed to tell him, of course."

"I don't remember telling him anything."

"Not surprising, but you did; enough for him to know – apart from what he could see for himself – that it was a matter for the police. Then he rang Luke, who flew back at once, after which you wouldn't believe the goings-on! It was like something on television! The police sealed the flat, sent in a forensics team, took away the clothes you'd been wearing to search for DNA and blood samples and issued a warrant for Rory's arrest! No polite nonsense about needing him 'to assist with enquiries'. He's a wanted man." Lady Sutherland paused in a way that Fiona knew meant more to come. "What he administered was a punishment beating; one of the doctors told the police that he'd treated your type of injuries when he was a registrar at a hospital in Belfast. But why, darling? That's what I can't understand. What would make Rory go berserk at this late stage?"

Fiona told the truth, but not the whole truth. "He said he owed me; that it was pay-back time. You know what a bad loser he is. He also told me he was not disposed to see *his* wife marrying some oil-rich American."

"Doing his usual dog-in-the-manger act," commented her mother thinly, "which has now become a vanishing act. I think someone's hiding him, though for the life of me I can't think who, or why, come to that – except his mother, of course, but I happen to know she's out of the country. Now then, is there anything I can do for you? Anything you'd like? I'm under orders from Luke to supply your every want."

"Do you know what I would love right now? A nice hot cup of tea . . ."

"Then you shall have one."

She also managed to eat some lightly scrambled egg and half a slice of hot, buttered toast, but it was slow going, and after swallowing the last bite she promptly fell asleep again.

When she awoke once more it was to find Luke sitting where her mother had been. Her response was to offer him her very best smile, ignoring her protesting ribs and holding out her arms as wide as she could. He was tenderly careful of her, but his embrace was still that of a man who once more had the world in his arms. For a long time they just held each other, aware of how lucky they were, then Fiona said on a deep thankful sigh: "Oh, how I needed that . . . you will never know how much . . ."

"Oh, yes I do . . . I thought I'd lost you . . . would

never get to hold you like this again." He put her away slightly so as to look into her eyes. "I can stand losing the baby; I could never have stood losing you." Carefully he gathered her close again. "We can have other children," he announced, in confident mode. "I've talked to the doc; he says that once you're healed – mentally as well as physically – there's no reason why we shouldn't strike it lucky again." His smile was the crooked one she loved. "Seems we hit the brass ring first try. Doc told me you were about eight weeks along. That places it at Thanksgiving." Raising a blond eyebrow: "You *were* going to tell me?"

She knew that glint in his eyes. It meant he was teasing.

"I'd only just found out for sure, and I planned to make the news one of your wedding presents . . ." Her eyes suffused. "I'm so sorry, darling. I wanted to give you this baby so very much." At the thought of what she had lost she burst into racking sobs. "It was awful . . ." she wept. "He'd used his fists on me more than once when we were married, but this time he used his feet as well! He kicked me as if I were a dog, only he was the rabid one. That's why I lost the baby . . . His aim was to hurt me, and you too, through me – he hates us both so much . . . He laughed when he told me he'd make me a battered bride . . ."

Over her head Luke's eyes were infernos, but he capped the volcano of his rage to say, a wealth of love and reassurance in his voice: "Battered or not, I love you. I always will love you. There is nothing he could do that would turn me away from you. Nothing. I will help you through this and back to your old self. We will both come

185

through it stronger than ever. You'll see . . . And when they catch him he'll pay for what he has done. In spades. I'll make sure of that . . ." He held her until the storm had passed, drying her tears, kissing her drowned eyes, until she was reduced to no more than dry heaves. Taking the second handful of tissues he held out, she blew her nose before sniffing: "Not so much of the old."

Luke's laugh was exultant at this welcome sign of the return of the sassy woman he had fallen in love with. "More your young self, then," he grinned. "There's life in your eyes again and your voice is stronger. Your mother told me you were amazingly lucid and calm considering what you went through." He regarded her from under his lashes before saying casually: "I talked to another of the docs on your team, the one who specialises in trauma . . . He suggested it might be a good idea for you to see a psychiatrist, since you've had the kind of traumatic experience that needs to be explored and understood."

Fiona reared, as he had known she would. Another welcome sign that her spirit level was rising. "I understand it only too well," she retorted in her Lady Bracknell voice. "I don't need any psychiatrist to tell me how to think. We Brits don't share your American tendency to run for therapy every time you break a nail or stub a toe!"

"OK, OK . . ." Luke concealed his relief as he held up his hands in mock surrender. "But this was no broken nail and you know it."

"Who better? But I'd still prefer to work through it in my own way. And with you. You are all the psychiatrist I

186

need, Luke. You and the enormous support and reassurance you constantly give me. I love and trust you with
all my heart because you are a *good* man, and right now I
need some goodness from a man, otherwise I will never
be able to bring myself to love and trust any man again."

Her voice cracked and once more he gathered her to
him. "You've got me," he vowed. "There's no way you
could ever get rid of me now; not since for a while it
seemed you wouldn't be around to so much as get to try
. . . He really worked you over, the bastard. If Charlie
hadn't come by when he did you'd have died. Thank God
he needed to know that access code."

Fiona's warning bell rang. "Access code?"

"Of course, I don't suppose you remember . . . He
told me you were drifting in and out of consciousness
while he waited for the ambulance. But that's why he
called on you. He had a dinner-cum-meeting with a
client and wanted to go through the file beforehand.
Only he couldn't get into its folder because he couldn't
remember the access code. Since the only thing elephan-
tine about you is your memory he checked the whereabouts book, saw where you were and headed over to
ask you."

Fiona examined that. "Why didn't he phone?" she
asked cannily.

Luke gave her an old-fashioned look. "You know my
rules as to the confidential numbers game . . ."

"Never reveal computer codes over an open telephone
line . . ." Fiona chanted obediently, thinking, So that's
what he told you. Clever, clever Charlie. The perfect alibi
and one you'd accept without question. "You're right, I

187

don't remember much about it," she fibbed – just about everything that had been done and said that afternoon had been engraved on her memory, trauma or not. But now was not the time. "I recall him kneeling by me . . . he kept wiping my face, and held my hand when the pain came . . ." She looked into Luke's eyes and told him truthfully: "I owe him my life . . ."

"You and me both," agreed Luke, and something fervent about the way he said it rang the bell of Fiona's curiosity. She looked at him expectantly, but he didn't take it further.

"Where is he anyway?" she probed. "He hasn't been to see me."

"He came with you to the hospital so that he could tell me where and how you were as soon as they told him, and he stood by until I got here. Later visitors were restricted to your mother and me while you were on the danger list. I also had you guarded, just in case Ballater tried to return to finish the job. He was obviously crazy enough to try it."

Fiona shook her head. "He won't come back now. Not when I'm alive and getting well and able to point the finger. He'll be under cover somewhere, but even he can't hide for ever. Mummy told me you have people out looking for him."

"I did," Luke admitted.

"Did?"

The way he looked at her had Fiona sitting up, wincing before asking incredulously: "They've found him?"

"Yes." Pause. "They found him all right." Another, longer pause. "But he was dead."

Fiona fell back against her pillows and stared at him until the shock faded. "*Dead!*"

Luke nodded. "It just so happens he was found this very morning at around nine, after a whole raft of people turned up at a house in Eaton Place to open it up for the owner, who's due back tomorrow after a long trip abroad. They were there to take in various deliveries, one of which was a truckload of liquor. It was when they went to put it away that they found Ballater. Lying at the foot of the cellar stairs. He'd been there for several days. His neck was broken. Evidently he had been drinking heavily and first consensus is that he was so drunk he lost his footing while going down the stairs and fell the rest of the way. The post-mortem will find out for sure."

Utterly taken aback by this sudden ending to what she had believed would be a long and winding trail, Fiona was silent until she had processed the information before asking: "Are they investigating his death?"

"What do you mean – investigating? What's to investigate?"

Over the months she had worked for him, got to know him and come – without realising it – to love him, Fiona had learned to read Luke, not least that expressive Western drawl. She had sat in on countless meetings, discussions and conferences – with clients, rivals, competitors, even possible partners – learning to decipher not only the tone of his voice but his speech patterns. Like the way in which he had just said, "What's to investigate?" She read that as meaning "Nothing, if I have anything to do with it."

So she said, laying the trail she wanted him to follow,

"There's always a police investigation into cases of sudden death. To find out how it happened."

"They know how it happened. He'd been drinking steadily for a week, was probably still stoned to the gills when he went for fresh supplies, lost his balance on the cellar steps and did a Humpty Dumpty. End of story. Five will get you ten thousand that the post-mortem will confirm every word I've said."

That's because the pathologist will lack one vital piece of information, Fiona didn't tell him. Which is that when I was married to Rory I often watched him drink hard-headed men into senseless heaps under the dinner table, while remaining rock steady on his own two feet. She searched Luke's face – as expressive as his voice and eyes – but he guilelessly met her gaze with the tolerant air of someone who couldn't understand why she was questioning the obvious.

Except that what was obvious to her was that for the first time in their relationship Luke was not being entirely truthful with her. Which dismayed her more than somewhat because it was not like him. Not like him at all. She had never known him to lie to her, whereas with Rory it had been second nature. Luke's honesty was one of the things she cherished about him, which was why she was at a loss to understand why he wasn't being honest now. Or what it was he wasn't being honest about.

She listened very carefully to his voice as he went on: "The police found a dozen empty whisky bottles in the room Ballater had been using, premier single malts every one. There was also a litter of empty winebottles – first growths every one of them. The cellar in that house contained some great vintages and it seems he'd been working his way through them."

Now that I *can* believe, thought Fiona, before asking: "Whose cellar was it?"

"Would you believe his mother's?" At her expression: "True . . . She's the one the house was being readied for. She's due back from Australia tomorrow."

"Of course . . ." Fiona appreciated. "Where else would he go but home to mother? She always bailed him out of trouble. Which is no doubt why he expected me to always do the same . . ." Then, on a frown: "Eaton Place, you said? She lived in Cadogan Square when I knew her." Her expression cleared as she found the answer. "Of course . . . Since then she's gone through another divorce and remarriage. No doubt Eaton Place was part of the spoils. I've never known her to leave a marriage empty-handed – unlike her son . . ."

"I don't give a damn about her or her misbegotten son." Luke's easy drawl had changed to the deadly, ice-cold one he used when confronting someone who had tried to do him down. "I'm glad he's dead. I'd have killed him myself if I'd been lucky enough to have the chance, and felt no guilt. Him breaking his neck is a godsend as far as I'm concerned. It means that I won't have to keep looking over my shoulder, wondering when next he's going to come out of the woodwork to try and finish you off. As far as I'm concerned his death sets us free. He was an off-the-wall son of a bitch and I hope he's in hell and burning for what he did to you . . ."

Which was when Fiona's ever-questioning mind turned up another nugget. Luke saw Rory's death in terms of "Vengeance is mine, saith J. J. Lucas." He had talked about *her* trauma, but while she had been hovering between life and death he had been undergoing his own. The moment she had been able to take notice she had picked up the strain in his face, the lines that were more deeply engraved, the shadows etched around his eyes, even – she saw now with a pang – grey hairs among the blond ones. These past few days had put him through the kind of emotional suffering no man should ever have to undergo once, never mind twice.

Which brought her to Charlie's cleverness in concocting the perfect revenge by remote control. Luke had destroyed Stella, Charlie's unattainable love, ergo Luke had to suffer the same shattering loss, all the more satisfying because it was his second – and last if Charlie had anything to do with it – chance. And yet – and this was where it all left the tracks and had her wandering round in a daze – Charlie had saved her life. Why had he not just checked – because that was the real reason for his visit to the flat – seen to his satisfaction, then walked away? Left her to die. That would have sealed his revenge. So why had he not taken it? Why had he stayed with her, called the ambulance, acompanied her to the hospital, called Luke then waited with her until he arrived?

Even as she framed the question in her mind, insight went off like a flashgun. *That's what Luke isn't telling me,* she thought. *Rory's death has to do with why Charlie changed his mind.* Luke knows why, but for some reason doesn't want to tell me.

She listened acutely to him saying with savage self-recrimination: "I feel this whole damned thing is partly my fault for not taking better care of you. I ought to have known that flaky creep wouldn't stay down no matter how hard I socked him. You should have had been under my protection *before* you were in hospital . . . not after!" – at which her suspicious mood did a somersault to one of remorse. God but you're a selfish bitch! she berated herself. Stop playing Miss Marple and give some thought to what Luke has gone through. Which thought prompted a memory of him sitting slumped by her bed, drowning in despair. If he isn't telling me something then it's for my own protection, she decided stoutly, placing a palm over his mouth before saying firmly: "You are not to blame yourself for what Rory did. How could you know that he'd do his nut? It never occurred to *me*, and if anyone should have twigged I should have!"

But Rory only did so because Charlie fed his paranoia, her inner voice prompted. So why did Charlie do a volte-face and decide to play Good Samaritan instead of Devil's advocate?

"I still should have known better," Luke was saying. "But I learn from my mistakes. It won't happen again. Trust me . . ."

"With my life," Fiona told him simply.

After a while: "When you feel up to it the police would like to talk to you about what happened, but as Ballater is now dead so is the case . . . There's no one to prosecute and not much more they can do except collate the facts before closing their file."

You hope, Fiona thought, accurately reading his voice again.

*   *   *

193

She gave her statement to a detective sergeant, recounting everything she remembered of what Rory had said and done on the afternoon in question, and why. She confirmed that he was a heavy and habitual drinker, that he was insanely jealous, had a violent temper and that during their marriage had beaten her more than once, the last time badly enough to cause the miscarriage which had sealed her resolve – terror of him or not – to seek the divorce he had never accepted. When she was asked why Mr Whitesky had called at the flat, she gave the version according to Luke. After which the detective sergeant thanked her, wished her well and left.

And then at last, Henry came to see her, carrying a square cardboard box, a flask and a massive bunch of roses.

"About time!" she reproached him lovingly. "I've been wondering why you, of all people, haven't been to see me."

"They wouldn't let me in before on account of you was too sick, and I been busy doin' things for Luke since he's been spendin' all his time with you. Anyway, now you can eat and drink real food I brung you some of my pecan brownies and some decent coffee. You need feedin' up."

With more than food, Fiona decided, as she returned his hug. The kind of sustenance I need from you, dear Henry, is information, but she fell on the brownies nevertheless. "Oh, Henry, these are balm to my soul . . ."

"After the goin'-over you had I reckon balm is what you need right now."

194

As she ate and drank, she watched him skilfully arrange the roses before marvelling: "A flower arranger too? Is there no end to your talents?"

"I watched your mother do it and asked her if she'd show me, so she did. That's a lady as knows a lot and don't mind sharin' her expertise. Now I know where you got yours from." He took the visitor's chair by the bed. "Luke says you'll be comin' home tomorrow."

Fiona's heart swelled at the casual "comin' home", but she said only: "Yes, thank God. I feel so much better now."

"You're lookin' more like yourself at that. Luke told me you got beat up real bad, and I can see where you did on account of you've still got the remains of a beautiful shiner and a fatter lip than I ever had when I was gettin' beat up for a livin'."

Fiona fingered her left eye, which was, even now, tender to the touch. When she had first been able to look at her face she had been aghast, for she was unrecognisable, her cheeks and chin discoloured and swollen, her lips the size of heavy-duty tyres and split in two places that had required stitching. She also had large haematomas on both breasts, while her chest and stomach were a mass of bruising. On finding her distraught and weeping, her doctor had reassured her that time and her own still-youthful healing processes would restore her to normality. Ten days later the swelling had for the most part subsided and the bruising was indeed fading, having reached that stage where the only colour remaining was yellow. Her doctor had assured her that too would fade. Her latest examination had been by the

195

obstetrician, who told her she was healing nicely, her internal stitching dissolving, but that it would be best to refrain from sexual intercourse for a while. She would know when she was ready.

Holding out her cup for a refill, she picked up yet another brownie before asking with cheerful innocence: "So . . . how are things back at the ranch? And what on earth has happened to Charlie? I thought at least he would come to see me so that I could thank him . . . He saved my life, after all."

Henry was silent, and the quality of that silence switched on Fiona's radar. "Henry?"

"He's gone all Cheyenne," Henry said finally. "Ain't left his room in days now. He don't eat – I leave trays since he don't answer when you knock – but they don't get touched. I don't think he's sleepin' either." He let twenty seconds tick by then he said flatly: "I don't think he expected what he found when he found you. Native Americans don't beat up on women. My guess is it set him to some serious thinking, and when Charlie does that he holes up behind a locked door and then goes inside hisself. I don't know where he goes but you don't see him and you don't hear him."

"A vision quest," Fiona said slowly.

Henry grunted. "Whatever."

With a trip of the heart Fiona fell into realisation and lay there, stunned. That was what Luke hadn't wanted her to know. And why Henry hadn't come to see her until now.

He had been keeping tabs on Charlie.

Who was on a vision quest.

196

It all came together perfectly, and the click as every-thing fitted into place acted as a mouse to a computer file, opening up all she had said to Charlie as they waited for the ambulance.

Things about Stella.

Things he had acted on.

"Luke says to let him be on account of he's got to work it all out in his own way since there ain't nobody else can do it for him." He refilled her coffee cup before con-tinuing: "He was the same way when Stella died."

Which confirmed Fiona in her belief. Luke knew – had always known – the real reason for Charlie's visit to the flat that afternoon. It also explained the access-code fairy tale. He had also known that Charlie was cultivating Rory Ballater because Henry would have told him. Henry was Luke's eyes and ears. That, as much as housekeeping, was his job. Who would pay any attention to a black American houseman-cum-cook who was al-ways in the background? What neither of them had foreseen was what would grow from Charlie's cultiva-tion. As Luke's guilt about leaving her unprotected had revealed.

The last thing any of them had understood was that Rory Ballater took no prisoners. Fiona had been meant to die, and would have done so had Charlie not found her in time, miscarrying the child who might have been another Stella . . .

Another Stella.

That was what had sealed Rory's fate.

And why Charlie was on his vision quest.

She had no proof, of course. What she was doing was

piling supposition on supposition. How had Charlie known where to find Rory? Unless Eaton Place was where Rory had made his HQ while in London . . . They must have met somewhere, after all. How else would Rory have known where to find her that particular afternoon? Charlie would have told him because he had checked the whereabouts book.

Not that it matters, she thought, since I have not one shred of provable evidence – no fingerprints, no forensic evidence, no witnesses – only hearsay and suspicion, neither of which is admissable in a court of law. There is nothing whatsoever to connect the deceased with an American named Charlie Whitesky except that they once took part in the same shooting party and attended the ball which followed it. Casual acquaintances, perhaps, but no more, and no reason to try and prove otherwise. As far as the police and the coroner would be concerned, Rory Ballater had been dead drunk when he had missed his footing, fallen down a flight of stone stairs on to a concrete floor and broken his neck. And as far as Luke and Henry were concerned, that suited them just fine. Charlie had atoned for his earlier actions, carried out the kind of justice they not only understood but approved of. *If* he had carried it out, of course, she reminded herself. Because she had no idea how he could have. She knew only that it must have been very skilfully and cleverly done.

Because Charlie was both skilful and clever.

And she had absolutely no proof.

Only knowledge.

And that too was inadmissible in a court of law.

One thing's for sure, though, she thought pragmatically. Luke's right: Rory's death – however it happened – sets us all free. Another is that, if Luke doesn't want me to know about it, it's because what I don't know can't hurt me and protection is the name of his game right now. The fact that he failed to protect me from Rory before has a lot to do with his tacit approval of what Charlie did after. And I can see his point.

But she still examined it carefully. Does it matter if Luke doesn't tell me the truth – whatever that is – about Rory's death? Or that I can never tell him that I think I know anyway? We will just have to pretend it never happened. After all, what matters is that Rory is dead; that he has been punished for murdering our child and almost killing me. Had he known I was pregnant by Luke he would have made very sure I died. Thank God nobody knew but me and my doctor.

No. Let's just say justice has been done and we are free of a blight on our lives.

She also had to admit, she told herself, that she felt absolutely no guilt. Only relief.

And Charlie?

He was something still to be resolved, she realised, but she had no idea how to go about it.

In which case all she could do was wait upon events.

She held out her cup again: "More of that perfect coffee of yours please, Henry. As always, it restoreth my soul . . ."

Lady Sutherland attended the inquest on Rory Ballater, as much to satisfy her own intense curiosity as to be able to give her daughter a blow-by-blow account when it was over. Because he had been the one to find Fiona, Charlie was called to give evidence.

"My dear! If you could have seen him! Positively shriven! As though he had been through an ordeal of some kind." He has, Fiona told her silently. "I never saw such a change in a man!"

"What did they ask him?"

"Oh . . . why he had gone to the flat . . . what time it was when he arrived, the state you were in, what you told him about what had happened and who had done it . . . Had he caught sight of anyone leaving? Met anyone on the stairs? – that sort of thing. But what clinched things was what the post-mortem revealed."

Fiona tensed.

"Rory's blood not only had an alcohol level that was off the scale, it contained enough cocaine to fuel an entire rave-up, or whatever it is they call those teenage parties. It seems he was an addict! They could tell because the inside of his nose was all burned away!" Lady Sutherland made a *moue* and shuddered. "Plus they found several bags of not only cocaine but heroin, in various hidey-holes throughout the house. They think he was dealing as well as using. No wonder he fell down those cellar stairs! How he could so much as stand is beyond me!" Her smile was pure *Schadenfreude*. "It was all one in the beautiful eye of the Archbitch, his mother. She's the one who ruined Rory; encouraged him to think that women were there for his use and pleasure, the way men are for her. Oh, yes, she was there – as if she gave a damn – glamorous as ever, swathed in politically incorrect sables and her usual indifference to anyone but herself. She actually had the nerve to cut me dead!"

Fiona was silent awhile, then said slowly: "So that clinches it then."

"Once and for all. But didn't I say there was something more than met the eye in Rory's overreaction? This drug thing explains it all . . ."

Charlie was her final visitor. She was waiting for Luke to come and collect her when he arrived unannounced, looking exactly as her mother had said. Shriven. The bronzed skin had a grey tinge and he had lost a lot of weight. No longer an irresistibly attractive, sexually devastating man, able to render women stupid with admiration and desire, this man was a stranger. He stood a little way off from the bed, proud, dignified, utterly removed from her by more than distance.

"I've come to say goodbye."

"Where are you going?"

"Back to where I belong."

Where else? Fiona thought. Formally she said: "I owe you my life. I was hoping you'd come to see me so that I could thank you for it." Deliberately she held out a hand so that he had to come forward to take it.

There was no flash of contact; her flesh didn't tingle, her heart didn't leap. No trace of their former "awareness" remained. It was dead. Like a lot of things, she thought. This closed, shuttered man who had obviously been through much suffering was not the dazzlingly handsome, urbane Charlie Whitesky who deliberately set out to seduce before carelessly abandoning once his purpose was served. This was Charlie Whitesky, Cheyenne, and he was going back to where that Charlie belonged. Oddly, in spite of what he had done to (and for?) her, she found she was fiercely glad for him, since back home on his own Indian territory he could come to terms with what he had done (*if* he had done it, she carefully corrected herself) and whatever (or whoever) it was he had sought on his vision quest. She only hoped it had been Stella, and that in communing with her spirit he had at last made his peace with the one human being he had loved.

"Will we see you again?" she ventured.

"When I'm ready." For "ready" read "purged", thought Fiona, because her reading of him, the only acute sense of him still working, knew that he still had a long way to go. Where to, only time would tell.

"I wish you well," she told him sincerely. "Good luck, Charlie. And thank you again." She paused before adding: "For *everything*."

Their eyes met and the message was received and understood, though his face remained impassive. He only bowed his head in a way that was at once graciously noble, innately proud and wholly Native American. "*Washte*," he said, in the old form, then left as silently as he had come.

Thirteen

When Fiona returned to the house in The Boltons it was to find it decorated as if for a party: streamers, a big WELCOME HOME banner, flowers and favours, American-style. There was champagne and Henry had cooked all her favourite dishes to tempt her appetite. She was more than ready to celebrate – there was so much to be grateful for, after all – so when at ten o'clock Luke picked her up from the sofa where he had insisted she lie, Roman fashion, to preside over the festivities, saying: "Doctor's orders. Early bed for the next few days," she was not inclined to go quietly. "Oh, but Luke . . . this is my party! The fact that I'm attending it proves I'm no longer an invalid." But she knew that look, that voice, and better than to argue, as she would have with Rory, who gave orders as a form of control. Luke saw these for what they were: necessary for her own good. Which meant that his own would come as a natural by-product.

So she did as she was told, which had her mother and Henry looking at each other with a "This *must* be love" lift of the eyebrows, and she enjoyed being held in a pair of strong arms and carried upstairs, where she found he had not only already run her a bath, but sprinkled it liberally with her favourite Jo Malone mandarin and lime bath oil.

Admitting to herself that he was right – as usual, she rejoiced – she luxuriated for fifteen minutes, enjoying the warmth and relaxation and feeling more than a little drowsy. When he returned it was to lift her out of the bath, wrap her in a sheet-sized towel and sit her on his knees to pat her dry. Ordinarily, that would have led on to other things, but he knew the rules as well as she did and, whilst his hands were loving, they were impersonal.

"What did I do to deserve you?" Fiona asked from a tight throat.

"Took me on," he answered simply.

Fiona looked into the mountain-snows eyes and knew that for the truth it was. With a relinquishing sigh she laid her head against his chest and closed her eyes, luxuriating in his warmth, his strength, his very self. "I need you so much, my love," she told him. "I need you to cleanse me of Rory's hate. You and I, we make *love* in all the ways there are, and love is what I need right now."

"You've got it," promised Luke. "As much as I've got. It's all yours. He may have tried to break your spirit but he failed, because it is unbreakable, like you. That's what I love about you – as much as I love everything else. What matters to me is that you're alive and well and here, on my lap and in my arms, where at one time I feared you would never be again. I always knew you were strong, but the way you're coping with this fills me with admiration. Whatever you need, if it is within my power to give it to you I will. It's a long time since any woman needed anything where I'm concerned, and I'm happy to give as much as I can. Whatever you want, Fiona. Whatever you need. In whatever form you wish. It's yours."

She did not reply and when he looked down at her he saw she was already fast asleep.

A week later they flew to a tiny island in the Bahamas which contained one small, pink-washed villa, plus a Bahamian couple to look after them. There Fiona slept a great deal, ate heartily, read a lot, swam daily, sunbathed carefully and, using Luke as her confessor, talked his ears off about Rory and the charnel-house that had been her so-called "perfect marriage". She admitted to him her fear of Rory's violence, and how that fear, allied to the stiff-necked pride of one both unwilling and ashamed to reveal the truth, had kept her prisoner for far more years than necessary. She also accepted that she hadn't been the right wife for Rory; that her argumentative spirit and quick tongue had acted like goads to a man who required submission in all things. She told him honestly all about her similar attraction to Charlie, and why, and how her past had kept her from making a mess of her future. She told him how love – real, true, honest-to-God love – had stalked her then mugged her, leaving her dazed and confused, and how her mother had conducted the post-mortem that revealed the truth.

She told him everything except the one thing she could not – would not ever – tell him, and she did it to protect him. She had long realised that he was determined she should remain unaware of and therefore untouched by any kind of complicity in Rory's death, because he also suspected it had come about because of what she had said to Charlie. Knowing only too well the deadly effects of guilt, he had resolved to keep her free of any taint of it by shouldering whatever responsibility there was. As he saw it, he had failed to protect her from Rory's spite. The least he could do, therefore, was to protect her now. And always, she realised lovingly.

So each in turn protected the other and lied by omission.

But he did tell her about Stella. All she had long wanted to know. About how she had been only a baby when she came with her brother to the Double J Ranch; how they had grown up together as brother and sister until the pigtailed little girl had turned into a lovely, raven-haired teenager, when his brotherly love underwent a chemical change and developed into the kind a man feels for a woman he wants to spend the rest of his life with. And of how his accidental killing of her had all but destroyed him.

And then, after they had been on the island ten days and were all talked out, the past exhumed before being reburied for good, Fiona's libido stormed back to clamorous, amorous life. Joyfully she made it clear to Luke that their enforced celibacy was over and with rapturous joy they gave themselves back to each other in an explosion of simultaneous passion which sealed their commitment for ever.

Which was when her recovery really began.

So it was with a feeling of blissful yet anticipatory relief that she awoke on the morning of her wedding day. She was healed physically, her face back to normal, all bruises faded, her internal stitching healed. She had regained the twelve pounds she had lost and was now

able to sleep without nightmares because each time she
had woken in terror Luke had been there for her: to hold
and soothe and demonstrate that she was safe, would
always be safe, because he would always be there for her.

She had come to love him, if that were possible, even
more deeply. Where Luke was concerned, love was a
daily revelation; not only physically – though that was
glorious – but emotionally, because in him she had found
a man who not only kept his word but lived up to his
responsibilities. She had never known the luxury of that
before and it bound her to him with threads of steel.
There was nothing she would not do for him, and the one
item she made sure went into her dressing case was the
rose-red silk nightgown of blessed memory, freshly
scented with Joy, to be worn again on her wedding night.

Iain – who would be giving her away – Moira and the
twins had arrived two days ago; Hamish had managed to
wangle a week's leave so as to act as an usher; and Henry
had baked the three-tier cake – soft sponge as it was an
American wedding – which he also decorated, again in
American soft icing. A knock on her door heralded him,
bearing her breakfast tray.

"Mornin'! You got a fine day for it. Sun's shinin' fit to
bust, though it's more than a mite cold." His grin all but
split his face. "Not that you need to worry. You got your
love to keep you warm."

"Ain't that the truth!" sparkled Fiona. "How's the
groom?"

"Rarin' to go. He sent you a message – on the tray. I
made your favourite, blueberry pancakes, and after them
you got the hairdresser at ten thirty."

On the breakfast tray he placed over her legs standing next to the coffee-pot, was a crystal flute containing one perfect red rose, tied to its stem was a tiny package. Opening it up, Fiona found a small velvet box. It contained a pair of earrings: diamond roses to match her clip.

Her eyes welled and her throat ached. Dearest, darling Luke. There never was and never would be a kinder, more thoughtful man. She loved him so much it hurt. Nothing like what she had felt for Rory and then Charlie. With those two men she had been in lust. Luke she *loved*.

At twelve fifty-five she was taking a last, critical look in her pier-glass when her mother knocked and entered. Seeing her daughter she said drily: "I came to see if there was anything I could do to help, but it's obvious you have got everything you could possibly want. I have never seen you look so lovely, darling."

"How I look reflects the way I feel. Indecently happy. Never in my life have I felt so – so – uplifted. Is that the word? Floating far above the world and looking down, knowing that with Luke to hold me I will never fall . . ."

"Yes . . . uplifted is the right word, because Luke will never let you down . . . Now, turn round and let me make a final check . . ."

Fiona did a slow turn, conscious that her face was restored, her body once more rounded and curvaceous, her dress perfection. It was a Valentino, of pure silk jersey, softly but intricately cut and draped so as to cling to the body yet flow over it, high at the throat and taut at the curve of the breast, smooth at the hips before falling away in subtle folds to just below the knee. It moved as she did, catching the light to gleam dully, its colour a true old-rose. A cloche of velvet roses in the same colour covered her hair, which had been dressed close to her head so as to expose the lovely bones of her face and her now unblemished skin. Luke's earrings glittered, matching the pin at her throat, and her high-heeled pumps were of silk dyed to match the dress. Long suede gloves of the same old-rose completed the whole, around which eddied the fragrance of Joy, both real and perfumed. Not a sentimental woman, Lady Sutherland was nevertheless moved when she said: "It may have cost the earth, but it was worth it!" Embracing her daughter: "This time it's right, darling. I have absolutely no doubt: Luke is the one for you."

"Talking of the groom, where is he?"

"Hovering."

"Give him a push in my direction."

"You're not superstitious?"

"I observed that superstition last time and look where it got me!"

He stood in the doorway, unusually elegant in a dark grey suit, blond hair gleaming, and Fiona saw the freshwater eyes glitter as if struck by sunlight, heard his intake of breath.

"Wow! You knock me off my feet!"

"No . . . that comes later." Fiona went to him. "Notice the earrings?"

He removed one to put his mouth to her ear, running his tongue around the delicate convolutions, making

Fiona turn his face so as to avidly capture his mouth with her own.

Then someone knocked and Henry's voice called: "This is your best man tellin' you the cars is waitin' at the front door."

Fiona stood back, her hands taking hold of Luke's. "Come on," she said. "Let's go get married."

Epilogue

One year later, to the very day, Lady Sutherland slowly and carefully descended the big, cantilevered staircase that rose from the vast floor-to-ceiling living room of the Double J Ranch, carrying with infinite love and pride a shawl-wrapped bundle. Seeing her, Luke halted his metronome pacing in mid-stride to regard her with a churning mixture of dread and anticipation. Her answering smile was radiant as she swept up to him, holding out the tiny bundle.

"Allow me to introduce you to your daughter," she said. "All of eleven minutes old and weighing a hefty seven pounds and eight ounces."

Luke accepted her offering as if it was the Holy Grail. "Fiona?" he asked anxiously.

"Dead tired but absolutely delighted. You can go up now, but first you have to see what all her labour was for." Lady Sutherland moved aside the folds of the cobwebby shawl, enabling Luke to see the baby. "Isn't she beautiful?"

But he could not answer, could do nothing but gaze at his daughter. She had a mass of fine, red-gold hair, and darker red lashes lay on the rose petals of her cheeks like feathers. As he gazed, she yawned hugely and raised them to reveal eyes like freshly watered purple pansies.

"Mine?" he managed incredulously.

"All yours." His mother-in-law kissed his cheek warmly. "Well done, Luke. She's going to be a beauty – and tall, like you. She measures twenty inches! And notice the hair: a real strawberry blond. Fiona was a very pretty baby, but your daughter is a stunner."

"Like her mother," Luke said besottedly.

"Why not go upstairs and tell her so?"

She watched as Luke, walking on eggshells, carefully toted his bundle across the room to take the stairs one at a time. Then she gave a contented sigh and went to tell Henry to open the champagne.

Fiona was also content, if tired. The baby had not been due for another five days, so it had been a surprise, to say the least, when she had found herself sitting in a puddle at the breakfast table as her waters broke. Prepared as he had been by not only her but the Lamaze classes they had attended together, he still found the reality alarming. All through her pregnancy he had kept her wrapped in cotton wool, mindful not only of the traumatic events of her last one, but of Stella and her triple loss. At times, his over-protectiveness had made Fiona want to scream, but she had set her teeth because she understood his fears.

They had settled into marriage comfortably now, but after their dream wedding the past year had not been roses, roses all the way. They had had their rows, their sulks, their stiff-necked silences, arguments that went up hill and down dale. But they had always eventually made it up in a way that added a fresh layer of cement to their relationship – which Fiona's ensuing pregnancy set on a plinth.

Fortunately Lady Sutherland, having arrived only that weekend, had taken charge in her brisk, authoritative way, telephoning the doctor, who said he'd be there as soon as he could, only to have Luke drive off at speed to collect him personally. He came back with not only the doctor but his nurse. Lady Sutherland told them that everything was proceeding normally and in her opinion, as someone who had undergone the experience three times, it would be some time yet before Luke was a *de facto* father.

He stayed with Fiona in the early stages, holding her hand and wiping her forehead, but as the contractions grew more severe he couldn't stand to see her suffer and needed no persuasion to leave her in professional hands. Once she was safely delivered, Fiona's first thought was for him: "Go and put him out of his misery," she begged her mother. Now, as he and his daughter came through the door of what Luke had set up months ago as a state-of-the-art delivery room, she felt her throat thicken at the look on his face. Carefully, he placed the baby on the bed before sitting down on its edge so that the infant lay between them.

"You approve, then?" Fiona asked.

He leaned over the baby to kiss his wife's willing and receptive mouth. "Thank you," he said fervently. "The best anniversary present ever."

"The whole thing would have been inconceivable without you," Fiona allowed modestly.

"Mine was the easiest – and the nicest – part; you did all the work." His eyes went over her and she saw the relief in them now that the sweat was gone, her colour restored, her pain a memory. "You sure you're OK?"

"Now I am, but at last I understand why they call it labour: it is indeed damned hard work!"

He put out a hand to touch her face, as though to reassure himself that she was still his warm, living, breathing Fiona. "I hated to see you suffer."

"But wasn't it worth it?"

Just then, the doctor came out of the bathroom, drying his hands. "Well, Luke . . ." He was an old friend. "A good morning's work, wouldn't you say?"

"To anyone within hearing distance."

"They'll all be here soon enough, but right now I want your wife to rest. She's used up a lot of energy. Let's go down and join your mother-in-law in a quaint old Scottish custom she calls 'wetting the baby's head' – except we're the ones who get the liquid. I'll give you five minutes."

The doctor departed, his nurse tactfully following him.

Left alone, they gazed bemusedly down at their daughter.

"What have we made, between us?" Luke marvelled. "I never really understood it until now – what it means to create another human being." With a look Fiona could have wrapped herself in: "We must do it again."

"I have no doubt we will."

"She's so incredibly beautiful – like her mother."

"Our next will be handsome – like his father."

The baby stirred, stretching out a tiny, star-like hand.

214

Luke put his forefinger against it and the fingers closed,
grasping strongly.

"Will you look at those hands? And those nails!
Miniature but flawless. She is the absolute in miracles."

"Miss Miracle Lucas?" Fiona winced. "Even allowing
for the peculiarity of American names, that is going
some. Besides, I thought we'd already agreed on Stella
. . ."

Luke's eyes met those of his wife and clung, his own
glittering brightly. "Have I told you lately that I love
you?"

"Yes, but you can always do it again."

As he lifted his mouth from hers: "I mean it," he said
intensely. "You saved my life. There was a time – before
you – when I thought all this" – he gestured to her and
the baby – "was lost to me for ever."

"Life's like that," Fiona said, as practically as she
could when all she wanted to do was howl. "It deals in
surprises, but only on its own terms."

"Now you tell me! Nine months I've waited for this
and I'm still rocked back on my heels."

"My pleasure," Fiona said demurely.

"And more to come." He kissed her again, his eyes as
clear as newly washed windows. "Now you rest, like the
doc said. I'll be back later, for longer."

"With a bottle of champagne, I trust. Save one from
that greedy lot downstairs."

"Henry already has it on ice – saved from the wedding." Smiling down at his wife and daughter:
"Best day's work you ever did for me," he complimented her.

"You don't do too badly yourself on the night-shift,"
she retorted saucily, and heard him laughing all the way
down the stairs.

Fiona drew her daughter into the curve of her arm and
kissed the rose-petal cheek. "Daddy approves . . ." she
told her.

Henry was already pouring the champagne, but Luke
had one last chore to perform. He had to summon all
hands to the celebration. "Lay on, Henry," he exhorted,
as he crossed to the windows, sliding them along to step
out on to the lawn and cross it to where a small rocket
launcher had been installed. Two rockets lay near by.
Picking one up, he inserted it, lit the fuse and stood back.
It smoked, fizzled, then whooshed skywards in a cloud of
white smoke to soar away into the heights of the deep-
blue, early-spring sky, against which it burst in a shower
of bright pink stars. All over the ranch, wherever the
hands were – with the cattle, rounding strays, mending
fences – the men looked up, saw the colour of the smoke
and knew it was a girl.

Up on the north pasture, from which the house
could be seen in the distance, Charlie heard the explosion and looked up quickly. So did the foreman he was
talking to.

"Well now," drawled the latter with a grin. "Looks
like we got ourselves a brand-new Miss Lucas."

Charlie was staring up at the pink smoke. He was
smiling, a fiercely proud shine to the dark eyes.
"Stella . . ." he said, as if tasting it. Then again, with
prideful joy: "Stella Whitesky Sutherland Lucas." He
clapped the foreman on the shoulder. "Talk to you

later," he said. "Right now I have to go make like a godfather . . ."

His horse was tethered to a fence about fifty yards away.

He began to run.